D1180241

THE THIRD EYE

Also by Etienne Leroux

Seven Days at the Silbersteins
One for the Devil

THE
THIRD EYE

·

ETIENNE LEROUX

Translated from Afrikaans
by Amy Starke

Houghton Mifflin Company Boston • 1969

Dedicated to Gloria and Hill Altepost

They all drank the toast eagerly.
They drank to the death of tradition and
primordial life. There was much gaiety and
freedom, and rejoicing without limits.

All characters are imaginary.
The story has been knocked together
from two works by Euripides and Sophocles.
The shopping center, alas,
is contemporary.

CONTENTS

THE TASK

Demosthenes H. de Goede, newly
promoted to the rank of Captain in the
Criminal Investigation Department and recently cured of a speech defect, of robust build and
a model of self-sufficiency, the embodiment of everyone's
Ideal Man, but with the handsome, serene face of one of mankind's patient servants etched with something of the sorrow
born of perpetual subservience to his calling, sat at his breakfast table eating noisily and sniffing through his nose, while
his wife, Hope, a nymphomaniac, looked at him with displeas-
ure. His gray suit fitted him a trifle too tightly. She nearly
went crazy with boredom every time she saw him relax after
one of his frequent jobs, and she suddenly thought: he used to
be able to move his ears. She said, "Move your ears." He did
so, and she no longer found it amusing. "Oh, Jesus!" she
groaned. She wanted to scream with frustration, but thought
better of it when she weighed it against his undisputed ability
in bed. Everything irritated her: his exercises at night for the
sake of his physique, his off-key voice when he tried to sing.
Once she ordered him to stop the exercises, and he developed
a paunch. She ordered him to resume them and managed to
put up with the irritation to her nerves until the paunch disappeared. No demand she made on him was too much; all
her nagging and accusations had so far not altered him; the
witches' dance she led him could not weaken him.

Hope had curlers in her hair and complexion cream on her
face. She felt miserable and could not forgive him for being
such a good person: so sensible in his decisions, so adaptable,
such a faithful servant to life, forgivable even when he mis-
used his power. She had deceived him time and again with

other men, and had elevated her feeble lies to the level of truths in the face of his credulity. She was powerless before his virtuousness, his itch to serve, his strong urges which satisfied her so delightfully, his capacity for patient struggle, his acceptance of any privation, his inextinguishable courage, his rages that could pass just as easily to gentleness, the unusual complexity behind the tantalizing simplicity.

She looked at him resentfully and longed suddenly for the sophisticated, aesthetic young officer who had been too modest that night at the Police Ball. She could not explain it exactly, but she felt vaguely dissatisfied with her lot, even though her greatest need was satisfied; her longings were based on her own shortcomings, and one sort of satisfaction most likely excluded another. She peered at him across the table like a vampire at an inexhaustible victim of the wrong blood group; or like something that had wandered out of the Middle Ages and did not understand our present day rituals of thaumaturgy. The four children, adopted by the couple after their frequent matings had proved to be fruitless, sat on either side of the table — curly-headed mites of uncertain lineage, with rebellious manners which, at this stage, probably disguised criminal tendencies behind superfluous energy. Two girls and two boys, ugly and vaguely alike. Their father, who had just finished his breakfast and now raised his unmusical voice in a tuneless ditty, good-naturedly suffered being banged by spoons and spattered with food from all directions. Hope's gown hung crookedly on her shoulders, exposing her large breasts. She lit a cigarette and scolded in the direction of the children, while she blew out clouds of smoke. Cold teacups stood on one side of the table and the remains of food congealed on the plates. Captain de Goede looked longingly out of the window where he saw part of the mountain above the house. On the summit was a massive pink cloud that was growing to alarming proportions — a deep rose-colored cloud that seemed to inflate itself to bursting point.

He got up and kissed Hope on her forehead, playfully pressing her breast with his hand. At first she wanted to push his hand away, but involuntarily pressed it closer. He leaned over and kissed his four children in places that were not too sticky, and then Captain Demosthenes de Goede went out the front door. When he had closed the door, he found himself in the small garden of his semi-detached house, right on top of a steep road. He looked at the mint growing next to the hedge and shoved the hose to the middle of the lawn. He closed the garden gate carefully and caught the bus on the street corner. He looked back and decided to buy the other half of the house for the sake of his growing children.

When he got down in the middle of the town and walked to a gray three-storied building, he hesitated in front of a smart Rolls-Royce parked next to the curb. A haughty chauffeur gazed straight ahead, the Royal Automobile Club emblem shone in the sun and the engine purred almost soundlessly under the hood. The commissionaire of the building said, "Good morning, Captain de Goede," and a well-groomed man sitting in the back of the Rolls-Royce immediately glanced up. He and Demosthenes de Goede regarded each other for a few seconds as though struck by the marked similarity in their looks, in spite of the trappings of class distinction, and then the Rolls-Royce drew swiftly away.

Demosthenes H. de Goede climbed the stairs and knocked at a door at the end of the passage. Everything smelled of the civil service, all the paint was a drab civil service color and everyone sauntered along at a civil service pace. The door was opened by a pretty girl who gave a professional smile and, having received an unexpected pinch, led him to a door where an effeminate young man with a superior air took over as guide. A third door was opened, and Demosthenes de Goede met Brigadier Ornassis E., head of the D-Service, in his remarkable sanctum.

2.

"Shall we come to the point at once?" asked Brigadier Ornassis E. "Thank you, James." He nodded to the effeminate young man who left the room, closing the door softly behind him.

There was a painting on the wall directly behind his head, and Demosthenes H. de Goede stared fixedly at it.

"Are you interested in pop art?" asked the Brigadier.

"No," said Demosthenes de Goede.

The Brigadier shrugged his shoulders.

"It's not everyone's cup of tea."

Hanging on the wall were a few early works of Max Ernst, Mark Rothko and a Jackson Pollock of the middle forties. Picasso's "Guernica" hung by itself.

"Reproductions," said the Brigadier. "You don't think I could afford the originals on a civil servant's salary, do you?"

"I don't really know much about art," said Demosthenes H. De Goede. In spite of having overcome his speech defect, he spoke very slowly, as though his thoughts emerged with difficulty.

"A man of action," said the Brigadier. "*Le parfait exemplaire de la vie énergique . . .*"

He was a slightly built man with the face of an ascetic who has seen a lot of trouble. The cut of his clothes was impeccable, his hands (now folded in an attitude of meditation) were soft and delicate.

"The ponos rather than the logos."

His gaze softened as he looked at Demosthenes de Goede with eyes that had acquired their expression of worldly wisdom from personal suffering.

"Are you happily married?" he asked suddenly.

Demosthenes de Goede's face brightened. He immediately took out photographs of the four little savages. For a long time the Brigadier looked with concentration at Hope's face in the background, her ripe figure — the promise of passion that is roused by blondes. Absentmindedly he listened to Demosthenes de Goede singing the praises of marital bliss while he opened a file and paged through it with his shapely hands.

He said, "I see you are the man who destroyed the Giant of Welgevonden."

"Strictly according to regulations," said Demosthenes de Goede, "after I had cautioned him three times."

"The Lesbian Poisoner of Calvinia, the Swine of Dysselsdorp, the Serpent of Muldersvlei, the Blackmailer of Arcadia, the Sweetheart of Kammaland, the Lion of the North, the Bull of Benoni, the Whores of Humansdorp . . ."

"I'm quoting press headlines, of course," added the Brigadier.

"There were many more," said Demosthenes de Goede with becoming modesty.

"You've certainly had a full life as a detective," said the Brigadier as he closed the file.

"It's a fight that never ends," said Demosthenes de Goede. "My life is full of hardships, and there is no rest."

"De Goede melancholikos," said the Brigadier and pressed a bell.

The effeminate young man appeared with a tray of drinks.

The glasses were repeatedly filled, and De Goede did not hesitate to swallow his brandy in great gulps under the watchful eye of the Brigadier.

"There is no rest," repeated Demosthenes de Goede. "It's one job after another. One has to pay to the hilt. You get dog tired and hardly ever see your wife and children. And I have never asked for any financial reward." He gestured to the Brigadier to add less water. "You just have to live from day to day — that's the only way you can take such a wearisome job."

The D-Service had no jurisdiction over the Criminal Investigation Department and Demosthenes de Goede felt free to talk in front of this little Brigadier whom he could pulverize with one blow. "In any case, I'll have to retire one of these days," he said. "I've got quite a lot of leave due me."

"There is still one task," said the Brigadier. "The C.I.D. has released you to us for it. It will be your last, because after that, for various reasons, you can be of no further use."

"I'm tired," said Demosthenes de Goede. He considered the Brigadier's words for a while and asked suddenly, "Will I be entitled to my pension even if I have not reached retiring age?"

"Certainly you will be entitled to your pension," answered the Brigadier softly.

They drank awhile in silence.

"Have you ever heard of Boris Gudenov?"

Demosthenes de Goede thought deeply. In his mind he ran over all the half-forgotten bits of knowledge from his police college days, and said, "The tyrant in Moussorgsky's opera."

The Brigadier and the effeminate young man, who had all this time been acting as a waiter, both laughed loudly. "*That* Godunov is spelled with a *u;* this one is G*u*denov and he is a tycoon."

He was still smiling, but then became serious.

"This will be your next task. To track down Boris Gudenov . . ." He was suddenly lost in thought. "To bring him to light."

Demosthenes de Goede put his glass down on the table next to him. He bored his clenched fist into the hollow of his hand, and it looked like a large knout. He sat erect, foursquare, with his eyes fixed on the Brigadier. His head seemed slightly too small for his body, but in spite of that he was still a handsome man: a huge lock-forward type, the South African hero par excellence.

"Perhaps I should first tell you something about the D-Service," said the Brigadier. He leaned back in his chair and eased his tie. "There is a great difference between us and the C.I.D. You catch criminals on the grounds of specific crimes committed; your Bible is Gardiner and Lansdowne's *Criminal Law & Procedure.* How can I explain it? Ours is uncodified. It is vaguer and more undecided. We really deal with spiritual crime."

The Brigadier lifted his hand to his silver-gray temples and covered his eyes while he concentrated. "We must protect

the community against spiritual crime, against the degeneration of the self, against the subtle onslaught on order, against
the alienation of established personifications, against the danger of the disintegration of the symbolic cosmos and the re-
sulting personal disintegration which reveals itself in all sorts
of acts of sabotage, in deterioration and the taking over by
demoniac and destructive forces. Is that clear?"

He opened his eyes and glanced sharply at Demosthenes de
Goede who had poured himself another drink.

"I am a simple man," said Demosthenes de Goede. "I only
know what I learned at the police college. There was a captain with us who had a yen for philosophy, but I'm not one for
all sorts of complicated fads and fancies." He took a sip. "Just
give me that Boris Gudenov alone. After I have throttled him
for half an hour, there will be no more mystery."

The Brigadier smiled. "It's probably the simple man who
has the most success — the man with vision, anger and gen-
erosity. He is the one who rises as the man of the hour, as the
savior, to restore the psychic balance of the epoch."

"He interfered with my wife," said Demosthenes de Goede,
sunk in thought. "The Police Captain, at the Police Ball one
night, and I smashed his jaw for him."

The Brigadier rose and stood in front of the "Guernica"
with his back to the Captain.

"There are some of us who are fated to sacrifice our personal desire for happiness and security. That, alas, is a fact.
Some people belong to the community and are expendable.
They are not important as individuals; their deeds are objective
and impersonal; they are all men rolled into one."

"I am a simple person," said Demosthenes de Goede, "and
many of these ideas are beyond me."

The Brigadier turned around and sat down again. "They are sometimes burned in the flame of creation."

"It's a lonely life," said Demosthenes de Goede, looking into his glass.

"They have to bring the mother of death to light and deprive her of her destructive powers."

"I curse the day that I was born," said Demosthenes de Goede, slow tears beginning to roll down his cheeks.

"They must disclose the shadow, exorcise it and make use of the creative power of the darkness. They must subdue the monster and harness its healing power."

"My mother told me when I was a child that I would endure much for the sake of my fellowmen," said Demosthenes de Goede while his tears flowed freely. "She said that I was born to all sorts of hardships. I have devoted my life to the C.I.D."

The Brigadier was disconcerted by the emotion shown by the strong man and gazed at him in fascination, meanwhile changing the subject.

"But to come back to the D-Service. All we have to rely on is the Suppression of Communism Act and certain other regulations, equally vague. Who and what is a communist?" He looked in vain for an answer to Demosthenes de Goede who had taken off his jacket and rolled up the sleeves of his white shirt to expose his hefty arms.

"Let's rather ask: Who is Boris Gudenov?"

Demosthenes de Goede now showed more interest.

"According to available sources, he is a tycoon of uncertain extraction. An immigrant from Poland or Hungary and a ruling shareholder in a large number of companies. He is a sort of Zaharoff, Gulbenkian and Gould rolled into one. He avoids all publicity, but is connected with more charitable institutions than any other person in the country. Oita, his shopping center in the middle of the town, is not only an architect's dream, but also a model of imaginative organization. You could be born there, live your life to the full and die there without leaving the building complex. *Life* describes it as a model town within a building."

The Brigadier was satisfied with the response his words aroused, for Demosthenes de Goede's forehead was creased in concentration.

"Name his crime and I will bring him to justice," said Demosthenes de Goede proudly, after he had struggled a moment in silence to formulate his sentence.

The Brigadier raised his hands and clapped them together. "My exact words were: 'bring to light,' Captain."

He meditated a moment searching like a priest for intelligible comparisons, but found no elucidating examples. He had lived for so long with the Gudenov image himself that he could no longer create any bridgeheads. Nowadays he could only think about aspects of the complicated personality. It was like having to discuss a difficult theory with someone who did not understand the basic principles.

He tried again. The Captain waited patiently.

"Almost nothing happens in this country that Boris Gudenov does not have a hand in. His influence stretches in all directions; his newspapers cover everything from Right to Left; his lackeys vary from rogues to divines; he is like quicksilver, always tantalizingly elusive."

Demosthenes de Goede once again considered a painting on the wall, this time the "Guernica."

For a moment it seemed that the Brigadier was helpless before the simplicity of the Captain's thought processes, and he himself, in a peculiar way, seemed a defender of complexity against crystal-clear simplicity.

"This struggle is like a dream," said the Brigadier. "There is nothing that hasn't a double meaning." His face cleared suddenly. "And your job is really this: to bring to light everything that is hidden; to disclose the monster; to expose the cobra to the sun . . ." He was forgetting his earlier resolve. "It is to wander down into the Unknown, the psychic substratum, and to make the Conscious triumph over the Unconscious . . ."

He stopped himself in time. For a few moments they stared at each other, two complementary personalities; one who had to formulate the job, the other to execute it.

Then the Brigadier came to a decision.

"All I want you to do is to find out everything about Boris Gudenov and report it to us. Even the slightest fact is important. Everything he says or does, or what others say he says or does, or whatever you hear or see."

Demosthenes de Goede nodded in understanding. He smiled suddenly, for he had expected a far more difficult job.

"And if I find enough evidence against him, may I take action?"

The Brigadier raised his delicate hands.

"In Heaven's name, no violence! You must not carry your revolver or use anything that may cause him serious bodily harm."

Demosthenes de Goede looked disappointed, but the promises in connection with his retirement and pension made him control his resentment. It would be an easy task.

The Brigadier seemed to read his thoughts. "It will be the

most difficult of all tasks — you are in greater danger than you think. And that is why it will also be your last work, for after that you will be of no further use to us, not even to the C.I.D."

The Brigadier weighed his next words carefully: "There is psychological danger attached to it. Your whole personality is at stake. Even you can become possessed . . ."

"I'm not afraid of witchcraft," said Demosthenes de Goede firmly. "In 'fifty-nine the Witch of Hillbrow . . ."

The Brigadier sighed and summoned the effeminate young man who appeared with his notebook, ready to write down the rest of the interview verbatim.

"Are you perhaps homosexually inclined?" the Brigadier asked Demosthenes de Goede, and raised his hands when the roar hit his eardrums. "It's important in the Service," he said. "For some reason or other it is more dangerous than hetero-sexuality."

He looked at the Captain attentively.

"You will have to change your style of dressing. Your suit is too drab. Your shoes are all wrong." He carried on a low conversation with the effeminate young man and then said, "A leather jacket and trousers not wider than fifteen inches. We'll let you have the outfit at cost price. The young lady at the door will fill in the forms for you." He turned again to the effeminate young man. "Loafers, perhaps?" and the young man nodded.

"No revolver."

Demosthenes de Goede's beloved Beretta was taken away from him.

The Brigadier shrugged his shoulders.

"You might perhaps find everything strange at first, but the

world of the D-Service is like that of a chameleon. We adapt
ourselves to our surroundings; we follow the spirit of the
times; we first melt into the background, then we strike." He
sighed and looked extremely unhappy. "Everything is for-
given the policeman and the detective, but the public can't
bear the Service to succeed. They write reams about us in
books and newspapers, but our presence in everyday life makes
them nervous. They feel that our existence is necessary, but
they regard our actions as immoral." The Brigadier's attention wandered off in renewed meditation. "Is it because we
identify ourselves with them to such an extent that we even
adopt their weaknesses?"

Demosthenes de Goede looked anxiously at his Beretta
which the effeminate young man was handling clumsily and
ordered him to oil it every week to prevent the barrel from
rusting.

Suddenly the Brigadier became brusque and businesslike.

"You will be known as H-12. You will report daily. Any
questions?"

"What does Boris Gudenov look like?" asked Demosthenes
de Goede.

"An intelligent question," said the Brigadier, opening a
drawer and taking out a photograph.

The Captain looked at it and frowned in an attempt to pin
down a fleeting memory.

"I've seen him before."

"This was the only photograph of Boris Gudenov available
to the D-Service," said the Brigadier. He inclined his ear to
the effeminate young man who was plucking his sleeve and
whispering. He stopped himself in time when, according to

Secret Service custom, he was on the point of burning the photograph.

"A remarkable likeness," said the Brigadier, studying the photograph again and looking at Demosthenes de Goede. He had now regained his former joviality. "A remarkable case." His imagination ran away with him again. "The inevitable struggle: the pursued under the spell of the pursuer; two aspects of the persona; two masks concealing one ego; Ahab and the whale in the turbulent sea of the Unconscious . . ."

Meanwhile he had taken Demosthenes de Goede's hand and was about to bring the interview to an end. "May it be of some comfort to you that in the dark struggle ahead of you your efforts will be accordingly elevated to the level of heroism, and the part you play will assume the appearance of tragedy."

Demosthenes de Goede just managed to keep his iron fist from crushing the flabby, almost boneless hand of the Brigadier to a pulp.

Before he left the room, the effeminate young man again whispered something to the Brigadier.

"Don't forget the function tomorrow night," said the Brigadier, "to introduce you to the Service. It will be quite informal, because, strictly speaking, we are dealing with an outsider. A minor gathering, perhaps, but still important for the purpose of making you feel one of us."

In the vestibule the attractive girl accompanied Demosthenes de Goede to the second door and, having received the pinch she was expecting, giggled joyfully.

Then she helped him fill in the form.

*

3.

"You look different," said Hope as she inspected her husband in his narrow trousers, scarf and leather jacket. "You look Bohemian."

On the way to the bedroom he told her about Boris Gudenov.

"Is he rich?" she asked, removing the jacket of her suit. "Is he young? Is he handsome?" she wanted to know as she dropped her skirt to the floor. Her mind was on Boris Gudenov as they began to make love.

At a certain stage their children came bursting in at the door and, screaming at the top of their voices, charged through the room and out at the other door leading to the lawn. Later on her questions began all over again. Would she get the chance to meet Boris Gudenov? Was he really a criminal? Whom did he look like? When her questions began to rouse even the sluggish suspicions of Demosthenes de Goede, she pulled him closer and made such vehement demands that his half-formed suspicions disappeared in the completion of his regular duty. The children thundered through the room a second time and Demosthenes de Goede, conqueror and martyr, protector of his house, provider of fruitfulness, orphan of the storm, relaxed for the time being next to his lovely sleeping wife.

There was only the break of a dreary Sunday afternoon between him and the tasks that were waiting around the corner. He thought of his mother who had said that his father had begotten him to endure more trouble than any other man. At that same moment, his wife stirred and stretched her limbs slowly while the children, scratched and torn, chased one another through the room again toward the lawn. When she was sleeping peacefully again, he thought of Boris Gudenov and tried to determine the nature of his task. He remembered the words of the Brigadier, and in his mind he challenged the specter, seeing himself as David matched against Goliath, the Redeemer in the struggle with Satan, the Crusader on the way to blessedness; and extremely fatigued, he took his Viking wife in his arms as, half-fuddled with sleep, she continued her unceasing demands. The children stampeded back through the bedroom, poor neglected scraps of flotsam reduced to tatters in their vendetta against one another.

The late afternoon melted into dusk, and the pink cloud crept over the mountain — a deep rose-colored cloud which exploded across the sky to become part of a multi-hued sunset. It was now evening, and the children, ragged and hungry, stumbled through the room to the empty dining room table. Their Viking mother awoke. She was fresh, and had completely recovered from her tiredness. She seized her giant urgently and hungrily. She endured his weary coupling, motionless and accusing.

"Heavens!" she said. "It's late, and the children are hungry. Stop it!" She bounced off the bed and dressed quickly. She was filled with longing for the romantic, demoniac, inscrutable Boris Gudenov.

She was a model of correctness as, prim and proper in her suit and blouse, she went to the kitchen to charge the servants with slackness.

*

4.

The afternoon before the function, Hope went to bemoan her lot to her mother, Madam Ritchie, who was spending the last years of her life in front of a transistor radio in the Welgevonden Foundation. At such an advanced age it was difficult to see any relationship between mother and daughter. The old woman sat like a mummy in a glass case, without any expression on her chalk-white face, and listened to Episode Three Hundred and Fifty of her serial, while the children climbed all over her. They tore her clothes, already strained over her swollen body, they knocked her wig awry and with the slightest touch left blue bruises on her snow white skin.

"Very soon they are sending him on a mission," complained Hope. "They are just making use of him." She was listening with half an ear to the serial. "He has to put up with anything for the sake of others." She seemed to be repeating the pattern of the story. "His half-brother inherited the family farm. His stepmother persecuted him all the time. He was an illegitimate child. The authorities make him do all the dangerous work." She rattled off her complaints while she ate cream cakes and slapped half-heartedly at the children. "He should never have been born. He should never have seen the light of day."

Her real grievances she kept to herself; she only grumbled about the acceptable injustices in front of the old woman, her senile mother, who, with her motheaten brain, could understand only one grievance pattern: the tyranny of authority, the incomprehensible ways of Providence, the cruelty of nurses, the restriction of regulations.

The old woman's mouth suddenly began to move, and she struggled to get the words out, but gave up the attempt. Her mouth remained open, then slowly closed.

Hope crossed her legs; she exposed a thigh through the slit in her green shantung dress and sniffed at a small bottle of *Capricci* perfume standing on the table next to her. She put it in her handbag and pulled at her bodice which was too tight. "He is very naïve," she said suddenly. "But he has the heart of a lion."

An hour passed while two more serials were dealt with. Then the old woman tried to rise. She could not manage it and sank back into her chair. She lifted her arm with difficulty, pointing to the wardrobe with her hand extended while a crooked finger, stiff with rheumatism, was directed inexorably to the floor.

Hope stood up, rummaged in the top drawer of the wardrobe and took out a small bottle.

Then the old woman spoke for the first time. Her toothless mouth and slack tongue found the word with ease. It lay in her mouth, it came slithering through a soggy marsh of lips, tongue, gums and palate. Underneath the discharge her eyes sparkled.

"*Yohimbin!*"

Hope danced a few ecstatic steps, followed by her children. She embraced the old woman while she kept her eyes tightly closed to shut out the picture of old age.

*

Demosthenes de Goede walked through the property of the Foundation to the cottage of the legendary Mrs. Dreyer, the fortune-teller. He passed the place where he had had the struggle with the half-witted Giant, and he proudly remembered his first triumph; he became sentimental at the stream where he had first kissed Hope. He saw the cottage where, in Mrs. Dreyer's imagery, he had found so many truths that were later confirmed. Under an oak tree a silver-gray Rolls-Royce was standing. The chauffeur's eyes were fixed on the upper branches of the tree on which hung bronze flasks, clanging against one another in time to the wind. The doves cooed softly among the leaves.

Demosthenes de Goede looked at the beloved cottage and saw signs everywhere of Mrs. Dreyer's success: her windows were decorated with gilt, the door at which he knocked in awe had a border of silver branches. As he waited he saw the doves in flight: the black ones from Thebes that had sailed into the world and the future and had landed in Ammon, Dodona and now, after so many centuries, here in the oaks of Welgevonden. He knew it was true — it was recorded in the Book of Life there in her sitting room. All her disciples knew it and were conversant with the esoteric wisdom of the Book. There was a whole chapter on the History of the Doves.

The door opened and he walked into the well loved room. First he put fifty cents on the table (the fee had remained unchanged through the years), then added twenty rand — the wonderful privilege of old clients who received the blessing of the whole truth from her lips. He noticed a thick wad of notes next to his and smiled proudly: every year he saw how her fame spread; every year the increased amount was proof of this. But this exceeded anything he had seen before . . .

A little later the door opened, and a distinguished looking man came out. A familiar face, thought Demosthenes de Goede before he brushed past him with a friendly greeting.

Mrs. Dreyer received him exactly as she had done many times in the past — as though she had never seen him before. Her plump figure was tightly encased in gleaming satin, her eyelids were purest gold, her makeup of the most expensive, her attitude aloof.

She studied the leaves in a Boche teacup.

"Are you related to the previous visitor?" she asked suddenly.

Demosthenes de Goede shook his head.

"Remarkable," she said, and looked out of the window at one of the black doves that sat seesawing on an oak branch and suddenly began pecking at a bronze flask in front of the bewitched eyes of the chauffeur.

"The end of your hardships will soon come," she said. "Were you abroad for fifteen years?"

Demosthenes de Goede shook his head again.

"That's strange," she said. "It's extremely puzzling."

She paid close attention to the tea leaves.

"You will soon be released of your burden."

But something was worrying her; she was obviously not happy.

"Have you any enemies?" she asked suddenly.

"Yes," said Demosthenes de Goede.

She pondered over the situation in the teacup carefully, and repeated, "There is release. That is certain."

Demosthenes de Goede waited for further revelations, but Mrs. Dreyer had apparently lost interest in him. He had never seen her so lovably absentminded as now when, having picked up another cup, she was looking from one to the other. He left the room quietly so as not to disturb her secret meditations.

He found the rich and important visitor still in the waiting room.

"She told me that I was destined to die within a short time or to spend the rest of my life in peace and quiet," said the man.

"One is not supposed to speak about it," said Demosthenes de Goede.

"I don't follow you."

"Did she give you a pointer?" asked Demosthenes de Goede. "One can usually pick up a hint in her voice."

"Why must one not talk about it?" asked the man.

"It's obvious enough," said Demosthenes de Goede.

They walked out of the room together.

"I can't remember exactly," said the man. "Anyway, the word 'die' is always louder than 'quiet.' Your voice usually drops when you say 'peace.'"

"It's the same as two people pulling a wishbone. You never tell your wish, because if you do it won't come true."

"Apparently she couldn't decide herself. And it's so easy to prophesy two extremes. Tomorrow you die, or you live."

They walked up to the Rolls-Royce, and the chauffeur tore himself away from the doves to open the door.

"Her words are usually obscure, but if you weigh them carefully and think about them, you realize later how true her prophecies are," said Demosthenes de Goede.

"Well, in my case both forecasts couldn't possibly come true," said the man.

"She foretold rest for me," said Demosthenes de Goede.

"She foretold rest for me as well, if I did not die," said the man.

"You needn't worry unnecessarily," said Demosthenes de

Goede. "She probably means that you will come to the end of your problems, whatever they may be."

"Perhaps the end of everything is the beginning of happiness," said the man.

"The end of everything can also be the beginning of death," said Demosthenes de Goede.

"Happiness can start with death."

"Rest can mean that the fight is over, and that you can live the rest of your life in peace on earth."

"Do you think that all one's problems become simpler in time?" asked the man with interest.

"She could have twisted the meaning of the words and meant rest when she said death, and vice versa."

"But then you are back where you started," said the man. "Even if you turn her words around and around, they remain a mystery."

"That's the Language of the Welgevonden Doves," said Demosthenes de Goede.

"Release may also mean death in your case," said the man.

"And rest may mean release in your case," said Demosthenes de Goede.

The Rolls-Royce rocked over the boundary of Welgevonden at eighty miles an hour.

"My wife and children are still with her mother at Welgevonden," said Demosthenes de Goede casually.

The man ordered the chauffeur to turn back.

*

There was great excitement when the children saw the Rolls-Royce. They wrote their names on the doors; they snatched the chauffeur's cap off on the way to town and they pressed the buttons that adjusted the windows. Hope sat between the two men with her eyes fixed primly on the road, but at the turns she took the opportunity of leaning heavily to the one side. When they stopped at the small semi-detached house and the man accompanied them to the door, she shook out her hair in the sunlight and laughed, showing beautiful white teeth.

"What a nice man," said Hope as the Rolls-Royce edged its way through the narrow little streets and the neighbors all flocked into their gardens. "Who is he?"

"I forgot to ask his name," said Demosthenes de Goede.

"We could try to see more of him," said Hope.

"He looks vaguely familiar," said Demosthenes de Goede. "I've seen a photo of him somewhere."

"He looks like you," said Hope.

"Obviously a man of good character," said Demosthenes de Goede.

He drank half a bottle of whisky while he shaved, exercized his abdominal muscles and dressed in the small stuffy bathroom. He cursed all the unpleasant tasks he had to perform, but his heart was really overflowing with love for his fellowmen.

In the bedroom his thick fingers had difficulty in hooking Hope's brassière in the third hole. The huge fellow sighed with pleasure as he saw his wife's attractive body tantalizingly disappear by degrees behind transparent nylon. What privilege, he thought, as her evening dress covered the most important parts from the common gaze. And for the first time he felt fit to tackle this unfamiliar task. He drank the rest of

the whisky and amused himself with isometric exercises while
he waited for his charming wife to finish painting her face like
a whore from Babylon.

5.

After the children had been fed and forced back into the
house, Demosthenes de Goede and Hope locked the door and
waited outside. Four enraged little faces peered through the
windowpanes and then one by one twisted with pain as they
began to bully one another — their only answer to boredom,
loneliness and frustration. They could see that a little girl's
nose had started to bleed, and one of the boys disappeared suddenly. Soon afterward Hope's budgie set up an unearthly cry.
"It's because you are so seldom at home," said Hope, primping
before the windowpane directly in front of a small strained
face. She smoothed her hair against her cheeks, turning her
head to see the effect from the side, in front of two icy green
eyes. "A mother can't do everything alone."

It occurred to her that she had forgotten her lipstick in the
house, and she unlocked the door at the same moment as the
taxi appeared and hooted. Demosthenes caught one of the
girls, who had slipped out in the dark, just in time and walked
back with her writhing like a worm over his shoulder. Hope
slapped her lightly just before Demosthenes de Goede closed
the door.

"Heavens! The children drive one mad!"

When they sank into the back seat of the taxi, she said, "Do
children ever realize the cross of parenthood?"

*

The lodge of the D-Service was designed by Cliffox, the avant-garde architect from the town, a contemporary of Carvajal. It was cylindrical, in the shape of a missile — a phallus pointing to the sky, a steel cypress among the Lombardies, a stainless supplication to the heavens. In the park wild buck grazed in the moonlight and under the stars.

Brigadier Ornassis E. welcomed them first, then embraced Hope — a liberty that was permissible on account of his higher rank and advanced age.

"Ah! The *charming* Mrs. de Goede," he said and remembered in time not to shake hands with Demosthenes de Goede. He introduced her to a group of willowy men dressed in the latest evening suits inspired by *Esquire*. Each responded with a charming smile to the cumbersome witticisms of their chief, while making Hope an elegant bow and nodding somewhat patronizingly to Demosthenes de Goede.

Hope had never seen so many good-looking men together before — there was steel in their litheness (no lack of courage here), there was the refinement which, through the years, she had missed so much. She looked at them with the eye of a connoisseur, but found it difficult in this strange setting to determine the measure of actual heterosexuality. She gave her best smile so that her teeth gleamed; false eyelashes partly veiled the light in her eyes and her full lips became soft and vulnerable.

"You must not be misled by their appearance," said Brigadier Ornassis E. as they walked into the hall where pot plants, bamboo mats and abstract drawings on the walls characterized the décor of the evening.

"*Outré*, isn't it?" he said, damning the decorations with a disdainful sweep of his arm. He led them to the main table where Hope took her seat on his right, Demosthenes de Goede on his left, and his effeminate secretary, James, and the rest of his elegant ménage in order of rank. A jazz ensemble was playing folk songs, and from time to time singers gave their renderings in the style of Trini Lopez and Joan Baez.

The Brigadier's eyes twinkled as he looked at Demosthenes de Goede who looked heavy and awkward in such select company. With a slight movement of his hand he summoned a merry blonde whose avoirdupois was visibly winning in the struggle with her tightly fitting evening gown. "We choose our corps not only for their intelligence, but also for their appearance," he said. "For instance, can you imagine anyone looking like Edward G. Robinson in a Secret Service today?" He took Hope's hand and raised it to his lips.

His silver hair suited him. His evening attire was old-fashioned. His superiority was based on personality, experience and the fact that he was the chief. He had reached the age where he knew how to turn even his shortcomings into assets. The fact that he was sometimes dramatic made him dangerous, an enigma to his followers.

Beautiful girls began to serve the wine. They wore their hair in beehives on their heads, their young breasts striving tantalizingly to emerge above their gowns, while their buttocks undulated under their tight skirts as they walked. They had a friendly smile for everyone and made the young men feel important.

"They are also part of the D-Service," said the Brigadier, clinking glasses with Demosthenes de Goede and Hope. "We recruit them on Clifton Beach. No special qualifications are necessary except the obvious, because they work on the sur-

face and save us a considerable amount of manpower by doing
small jobs that would be a waste of time for the rest of our
staff."

He was in a genial mood and looked approvingly at the
blonde who was trying out her only talent on Demosthenes de
Goede.

Some of the young men had already started to dance after
making a slight bow in the direction of their chief. They shivered and writhed with the girls, finding communication under
drooping eyelids with great hollow eyes staring at them from
under green makeup. The narrow skirts were alternately
creased and stretched by the suggestive and almost invisible
movements of the dance — those restrained movements that
were more intimate than the Frug gave a deeper more spiritual satisfaction hinting at a contained, more intense and greater
passion.

"We choose our members not only for their intelligence and
ability," repeated Brigadier Ornassis E., "but also for their
physique and general appearance." He pointed approvingly
to his young men busy dancing. "Our girls test them out like
Gnostic women, and immunize them in the process from any
outside temptation."

He lit a cigarette for Hope, stroking her cheek with his little finger. "There is nothing that the world of the Archons
can offer that these girls can't do better." He stole a quick
playful kiss from Hope. "Do you understand?"

Hope was in her element. She unconsciously copied the
girls, completely under the spell of the Service. She was cap-
tivated by a new idea: a fuller life, sex as a sort of religion, a
servitude that had meaning.

"Is this what I have been searching for all my life?" she whispered to the Brigadier.

At once Brigadier Ornassis E. became a wise old guru. His eyes became cunning. "Are you still thinking of the poetic Captain? Do you find these young men different?" He began to stroke her thigh lightly. "Are you afraid that intelligence always goes with effeminacy? Do you find the animus within you incomprehensible? Are you constantly misled?"

Meanwhile Demosthenes de Goede had led the blonde onto the dance floor where he whirled like a merry-go-round and lifted her lightly onto his shoulders, his booming laugh obviously unsettling the other couples.

The Brigadier smiled good-naturedly. "That's one of the reasons we chose him," he said. His mouth was close to Hope's ear and he playfully bit the lobe. "He is so utterly a man, so close to nature, so unlike the spirit of the times. And if we find his character so difficult to understand, how much more so will our enemies find it?" He sat back comfortably. "There is a complexity in simplicity for all those who are themselves complicated. Our greatest champions were always people noted for the simplicity of their faith."

Hope was not listening. She was now playing the role of the girls of the Service with whom she identified herself. She was entirely integrated into the movement. Her function was suddenly clear to her; she had found a meaning; she had discovered the outlet of self-sacrifice — a counter image of narcissism. The riddle in the looking glass which she saw every day was solved.

Brigadier Ornassis E. raised his hands to his eyes — his delicately perfumed hands.

"There is death in the building," he said.

He lifted her hand once more to his lips and kissed it lightly.
"And we can't fight it with camp and twee."

He made a slight gesture and the orchestra stopped at once.
They all gathered around the table. The girls brought wine
and smiled at everyone, making them feel happy. They examined one another with expert eyes for any deviation from
the group norm. From time to time they went to the powder
room where they pulled a neckline wider, made an eyelid
greener, hitched a dress higher or opened a zipper fastener a
little farther.

Brigadier Ornassis E. placed his fingertips together and addressed the group at the table.

"I can perhaps make a cursory reference to our organization," he said to Demosthenes de Goede who by now had the
disheveled blonde on his lap. "We have two lines in our organization: the personnel group and the action front."

He gestured to one of the attractive young men who continued slowly and clearly, but in a somewhat bored fashion.

"The personnel group are the men with ideas: they deal
with the image of the Service; they formulate the principles."

Brigadier Ornassis E. nodded, and another young man completed the elucidation slowly and indolently.

"We," he said, "well, we carry out the policy."

There was appreciative laughter from his group.

"And that," said Brigadier Ornassis E. to Demosthenes de
Goede, "is also your task." He pointed to the first young man.
"The specialized personnel group is limited to their function as
men of ideas — even if they are of higher rank. It is the action
front who have the most opportunities, in spite of the fact
that their function is limited to the execution of a task."

He pointed to himself.

"I am more or less a managing director. Together with the personnel group, I am responsible for the expansion of the Service. Perhaps I am the nearest thing to a tycoon like Boris Gudenov, although such a thing is naturally unthinkable in our organization. We are an incorporate entity, and I am also responsible to the state, and to society, for the results of the Service."

He motioned to the blonde to stop offering resistance.

"I feel perhaps more attracted to the personnel group, but I don't deny the importance of the action front. In point of fact, I (alas) am a sort of father figure."

He laughed aggressively and everyone followed suit. Then he raised his hand for silence and nodded approvingly when there was an immediate response.

"Perhaps it would be a good thing if we look at the struggle in this light: Boris Gudenov is the tycoon, the invisible power behind the scenes; Demosthenes de Goede is the one with the Service, the state and the public behind him."

The maidens of the Service had meanwhile also gathered around the table, and all were listening attentively to Brigadier Ornassis E.

"There is perhaps a certain similarity, apart from appearance, between the two . . ."

Hope opened her eyes wide, and the Brigadier gave her a light but substantial pinch just where her evening gown slid yieldingly over her leg.

"Oh, so you've seen Boris Gudenov before?" He put a cigarette between his lips and beat his men to it with a Ronson lighter. "Demosthenes de Goede is big and strong; Boris Gudenov is big and strong, but in a different way." He blew out a cloud of smoke. "I have often wondered: is there perhaps an affinity between the intellectual and the athlete?" He shook his head and moved his hands uncertainly. "Are Boris Gudenov and Demosthenes de Goede not both victims of something stronger than themselves? The tycoon in the empire of his own creating becomes trapped by loneliness; the hero becomes isolated by the persistent demands of his work."

He pointed to Demosthenes de Goede who, thanks to the Brigadier's orders, was now comfortably persuading the blonde to yield.

"One cannot regard him as very complicated. He remains preeminently human, in spite of his strength and his ability to endure suffering. Is there not perhaps in him something of all that we see in ourselves? A lyrical hero of Pindar; a tragic figure in spite of the comic side; a stoical patience and a natural inborn wisdom?" One of the girls who approached too close to the Brigadier was adroitly obstructed by Hope.

In the distance was a huddle of waiters in smart uniforms, but with a different sort of elegance from that of the gentlemen of the Service. Like all in their calling, they had become the reflection of the people whom they served but subject to the shortcomings inherent in imitation — the movement without personality, the gesture without meaning. Brigadier Ornassis E. called the headwaiter and whispered in his ear.

The girls of the Service, whose job of serving wine had now been taken over by the waiters, sat down on the floor, their skirts spread out like flower petals, their demeanor bashful, their arms ready to receive, one after the other, the young men of the Service who stretched out beside them, their faces raised to Brigadier Ornassis E.

"They say," continued the Brigadier, "that we are living in an age of anti-tragedy, of Christian and Marxist metaphysics — the two myths that, in passing, only take note of one aspect of tragedy — in a world that only recognizes victory in the hereafter, in the one case, and in the material world, in the other. But is this true?"

He turned to Hope who had the look of a woman in love who sees even in an unintelligible play of words a play of love; or of those women who have reached an age where they find themselves free of the limitation of a single defined love, where they all become nymphomaniacs, where a lonely nymphomaniac like Hope suddenly feels at one with all women and becomes quiet and submissive, and quietly gives herself in bondage to love.

"Is this true?" asked Brigadier Ornassis E. "Are there not in man's psyche uncontrollable forces, demoniac apparitions which can drive him to frenzy?"

He now addressed Demosthenes de Goede who was manipulating the blonde like clay and becoming hopelessly involved in her overeager concessions.

"Is it not true," asked the Brigadier, "that we have reached a stage where both the spiritual and the materialistic myths have fallen away, and man, without anchor, is capable of experiencing tragedy all over again?" He looked at the personnel division of the D-Service who were following him attentively. "Have we not again reached a pre-rational stage?"

The Brigadier was lost a moment in thought, while the girls, lulled by his voice and the music, leaned back in the arms of the young men. Then he straightened himself and motioned to the waiters who at once came bursting out of their own frustration at the swinging doors. They came pour-

ing from the kitchen behind the bamboo mats and abstract
drawings, carrying grilled uterine animals on silver trays,
brown shiny suckling pigs with glassy eyes. Row after row
they came, in impeccable evening attire, past the Brigadier
and his followers, through a second door into the next room.

The Brigadier rose and, with Hope on his arm, led everyone
to the Coronet Room, a conversation piece designed in the
neoclassical style, fitted with air-conditioning and livened up
by a continental orchestra playing soothing music for the
dinner hour. He sat at the head of the table, his guests on
either side, and waited with bowed head until the waiter had
poured a little Veuve Clicquot (Extra Sec) into a Steuben
glass. He studied the label, allowed the wine to sparkle on his
tongue and declared himself satisfied. Silently he waited for
all the glasses to be filled, then slowly rose. There was a hush,
the orchestra ceased playing, the waiters stood in serried rows
and the Brigadier lifted his glass high and said, "To the Beloved Maiden!"

The high-spirited young men of the Service sprang
promptly to their feet, and from every side the toast of the
evening rang through the room. "The *Kore*, the *Kore!*"

Hope found this "fantastic" and wanted to know what the
Kore was. The Brigadier explained that it was the legendary
Maiden. Demosthenes de Goede, slightly fuddled but bursting
with energy, roared that all maidens were doomed to be violated at some stage or other. The Brigadier nodded and explained that the psychology was quite correct: the one who
was violated was just as implicated, that defloration was a law
of nature, that virginity in itself contained the greatest temptation to dishonor. After that they fell to on the succulent
suckling pigs whose crisp flesh melted sensually in their mouths

— essentially a symbolic violation and the first step of self-satisfaction in the narrowing circle of self-indulgence.

When the tender suckling pigs had been dispatched and the dessert had calmed down the final tempo of the meal, the Brigadier again rose slowly to deliver the speech of the evening in honor of his dazed guest.

He referred to the stirring task of one like Demosthenes de Goede who worked, not for himself, but for the community; who sacrificed himself to solve the problem; who without personal consideration placed himself on the altar to represent our collective participation; who in these confused times appeared like an archetypal hero, to give meaning to the anxieties of the ordinary people and the unintelligible visions of our creative spirits.

He enlarged movingly on one such as Hope, the model mother of our era, who often had to forgo domestic happiness; who had, without the help and support of her husband, to bear the responsibility of her liberty; who had to reconcile her solemn right to emancipation with the absence of her husband.

Then Brigadier Ornassis E. became esoteric, philosophical and difficult to follow. With soaring volubility he described the work of Demosthenes H. de Goede as an attempt at the unification of our world with a cosmic world, where each individual had to discover his true nature in all that was hidden, and therefore unintelligible. It was the lover's way, the artist's way, the way of each one of us.

"And in this can we not see the image of our friend Demosthenes de Goede" asked the Brigadier, "as a kind of artist of deeds? And can we not see in Boris Gudenov, the hated enemy (because that is how I know him), also the perverted lover?

And can I not see all of us in the role of the lover, the artist?"

Everyone in the hall remained silent. Each girl looked tensely from under green eyelids, dedicated and submissive to the Head of the D-Service. The men, reconciled by the very nature of their calling to the mystery of the abstract, were equally silent, their attention as members of personnel and the action front riveted on their leader, the Brigadier, and on the possible implication of his words.

"You," said the Brigadier to Demosthenes de Goede, "are going where many of us fear to tread." Everyone now turned toward Demosthenes de Goede who sat and listened without moving, a frown on his forehead, rather impatient of all this verbosity, but flattered nevertheless by the attention he was receiving. "You are going, Captain de Goede, not just to make a bare display of strength in the name of the Service, but to free the world from a corrupting monster that has appeared out of the darkness and seized on our understanding; you are going to free man himself."

He picked up his glass once more. "You have drunk to the Maiden," said the Brigadier. "Gentlemen, I now give you the Hero of the evening."

There was loud applause when Demosthenes de Goede stood up and made his bow. They crowded around him as he embraced the girls and pulverized the outstretched hands of the corps. Wine flowed freely, and the Brigadier was proud of his gesture when specially imported blood-red *Sang d'Hercule* from Argos was served. It was at this moment that Hope seized the opportunity to take out her little bottle and slip, unnoticed, a few drops into the Brigadier's glass. She waited patiently for the reaction — the strain about the eyes, the quickened breathing, the flush on the face and all the other characteristic symptoms. She saw how the Brigadier cocked his head slightly, as though becoming aware of something deep within him; she noticed the swaying movement of his body, the signs of abandonment evident in word, gesture and the timbre of his voice. She was on the point of offering herself as victim, unwittingly faithful to the role of the *Kore*, when the Brigadier suddenly lifted his hand, bringing the orchestra to a stop, and with restrained slowness moved in the direction of the third room. On the way there he flung his arms tightly around his adjutant, James, and Hope was dismayed to see how the men of the Service, one after the other, abandoned the girls and together with Demosthenes de Goede, followed the Brigadier arm in arm.

The door opened, and there was a fleeting glimpse of the El Gaucho room with kinetic sculpture by Lye and Schoeffer, a third orchestra giving a rendering on cymbals of the *Poème Symphonique* by Ligeti. The door closed behind them, and the girls of the D-Service found seats on the chairs scattered about everywhere in small groups. They took out their knitting and calmly began to knit while they carried on lively suburban conversations. As time passed some of them dozed off while the men in the inner room were busy bringing the initiation orgy to a conclusion.

Hope, bored, wandered back and forth in the hall, and then began to dance by herself in time to the continental orchestra's "Fools Rush In." She rotated her hips and pelvis, lost in introspection, her heart breaking in the only tragedy she knew — the tragedy of waste, of lost opportunities, of moments that have passed — a lament, expressed in movement, for the enigma of life; a reverie in dance time on the squandering of life-giving energy, the wasting of precious libido.

EARLY HISTORY

Boris Gudenov, back from Lydia
where he served Omphalia with all his
talents and procured handsome dividends for
his shareholders · He had been abroad for fifteen
months, but had not managed, in spite of all the funds
at his disposal, to overcome the heat, the flies and the loneliness of Africa. Omphalia was a beautiful woman of platinum
and tin, her breasts were the mine dumps in the desert, her
breath the overpowering fumes of small pubs with the bottles
on Victorian shelves; her urges were inflamed by the fierce
warmth of early maturing women and her love affairs were
the legends in the brochures drawn up by the tourist guides.
Contact with her was dangerously infectious, her beautiful
eyes were misty with the first signs of optical disease, her nature was adaptable and obliging as the result of a different
conception of servitude — a surrender of the heart and not
the head. She smelled of *Chanel* and slept on golden beds
where she taught him all sorts of perversions: he dressed himself in her highly colored garments, while she fancied herself
masculine in gold spattered pants. He had to pay heavily for
all those dividends, and to stand up to the jeering of an ebony
Pan who peeped through windows and keyholes. Snow
white teeth mocked his claim to virility, so that one day, in
a moment of rage, he seized the arrogant youth and like an
old-fashioned Bwana flung him out at the door. After that
the mighty Boris had to bite the dust, and his reputation became the laugh of the place. He waited in palace anterooms
and listened to threats. It was his money, his know-how and
his technical skill that saved him, not his manhood. In pulling
him down she bore him fair dividends, but the mighty Gu-

denov's name had been dragged through the mud. They
mocked him further by riding around in Cadillacs that were
more ostentatious than his Rolls-Royce.

A rumor circulated that he was impotent.

He could not bring her to an orgasm.

He was an effeminate weakling who tried to buy everything
with money.

He was not even a good boxer or an athlete.

There was a stain on the Gudenov name.

They said he had stabbed his best friend in the back.

But worst of all was the rumor that he was a "fairy." There
were plenty of similar names that he had to live down: Nola,
pix, flit, queer, fag, faggot, agfay, fruit, nance, queen and she-
male.

*

*On his return Boris Gudenov devotes his attention to the
Oechalia Publishing Company and settles his account with
Ernest Eurytus.*

Without any compunction he had checkmated Eurytus and
ruined him utterly: an example of what is often cited in
financial circles as legal expungement.

Ernest was the head of a fine business; a little old man with
gray hair, proud of his beautiful daughter, Iole, and his son,
Iphitus, who at one time had been a friend of Gudenov's.
They said that he had known Boris Gudenov as a boy in far-
off Poland and had often helped him in times of trouble. He
had started with a small shop in the Little Karroo where he had
begun by selling blankets and sweets on the ground floor. Be-
tweenwhiles he had made a small fortune from ostrich feath-

ers — that was before the days of cooperative marketing. He spent his spare time reading on the second story of the rickety shop which he reached by climbing a spiral staircase and from where he could look out over a pepper tree and across to the great Swartberg range in the distance. He collected so many books that the shelves bent under the weight. Later on he established the publishing company in the town and set up his own newspaper. At first he supported the government, but when he became strong enough he launched out on his own.

Iole, the girl who had played with farmers' sons on the banks of the Olifants River, was "finished" at a liberal university and developed into a beautiful madonna with a social conscience which made her a follower of lofty causes. The color question, especially, captured her attention, and she devoted her time to the liberation of the intellectual African. The Oechalia press leaned more and more to the Left and the progressives, and the old man who had sold ostrich feathers could vindicate his past and at the same time gain an entrée into a circle which he had always regarded as inaccessible.

Iole and her father had once spent a holiday on the Côte d'Azur in a villa belonging to Boris Gudenov — arranged because of old friendship ties, and because Boris Gudenov had obtained a share in the Oechalia Publishing Company. The last evening there they had met again, after so many years, at a grand ball which Gudenov attended in person, having just returned from one of his business trips. Iole had immediately felt attracted to this handsome, quiet man with his cold, haughty, intellectual aloofness. They danced together the whole evening and drank champagne under the stars on a terrace overlooking the sea. He had kissed her for the first time and had not been able to forget the cool, damp lips of the maiden.

Back in South Africa and true to her upbringing, she had taken part in an act of sabotage in which three Africans and a white woman were accidentally killed. She was acquitted on the technical grounds of nonparticipation because of some uncertainty in the evidence. The Gudenov press had given a good deal of publicity to the case — mainly because Iole was outstandingly photogenic — without the knowledge or co-operation of Boris Gudenov who was far too exalted a personage to be worried with the local ramifications of his financial network.

It was a heavy blow to the old man who began to see the first signs of disintegration in his affairs. He was particularly cool to Gudenov after that. His son Iphitus, a homosexual poet, had tried to intervene and had made the mistake of justifying his father and playing off his sister's sensitivity to political problems against the heartlessness of capitalism that had claimed his ex-friend as a victim. Boris was furious at the arrogant attitude adopted by the miserable little milksop who had dared to pester him with banalities. When the rot had gone farther with the arrest of Iphitus in Government Avenue by a policeman called Coertzen on a charge of indecent exposure, and the Gudenov press had gone to town over the incident, the old man declared open war on the mighty Gudenov.

He threw everything into the fray when Iphitus shortly afterward committed suicide. He had nothing left: his affairs were collapsing under him, and he used everything at his disposal to seek revenge. There was certainly no man more hated than Gudenov in the Oechalia press campaign which coincided with Boris' trips to Lydia where his interests were threatened with nationalization.

Boris had returned with hatred in his heart and had wiped out the Oechalia Publishing Company. The government press had praised his take-over and, for the time being, Gudenov had become a hero in the eyes of the conservative section — against his wish, because Gudenov was Gudenov, and his appetite was not restricted to specified dishes.

The old man followed his son, because he found it beyond his powers to return to the hard reality of the Swartberg.

*

Boris Gudenov "takes pity" on Iole and engages her as his private secretary to accompany him everywhere, even into his flat above the shopping center, where Katy, his wife, by this time used to his "secretaries," waits patiently.

It was difficult to detect any change in Iole after the death of her father and the collapse of his business — as difficult as it had been to see any signs of emotion on her face during the sabotage case in which she was involved. She was slender, dark and very beautiful, almost unbearably so because her beauty was made perfect by the firm contours of youth, and her aloofness made her unapproachable. She was quiet without being timid; her pride only gave offense to her inferiors. It was difficult to explain the part she played in subversive activities: in that respect she was an enigma even to the liberal group who counted her among its members. The fact that sexual perversion and all kinds of depravity were mentioned

in connection with the sabotage group was difficult to reconcile with her madonnalike appearance and high ideals.

Everyone had his own ideas about why she placed herself
under the protection of the demoniac Gudenov after her
father's death. Some said that she was biding her time until
she could take a terrible revenge. Others averred that her
participation in sabotage and other undermining activities had
rendered her entirely amoral, and that she could never return
to normal standards again. Some saw in her surrender a romantic image of an old love that after all those years had come
into its own; but that was difficult to reconcile with our
times, and her age. She spoke so seldom; she was so unassail-
able; she was such a mysterious contradiction — the modern,
highly sophisticated woman, with the cosmetic mask of a
virgin: white lips, dark eyes and long hair hanging to her
shoulders. The problem grew, because everyone claimed
that he knew the real story of the tycoon: the one who chose
beautiful girls with intelligence, but of inferior social status,
to release him from his loneliness — girls who, in their basic
simplicity, had a better understanding of his needs and would
not burden him with psychological complications, who were
ready to be materially pampered without further demands
on the grounds of personal pride, who had enough sophistication to keep him longer than their better bred sisters who
looked upon him as a rival, who were willing to sacrifice a
small part of their youth as payment, who made no demands
on him with regard to extravagant physical achievements, who
did not try to "understand" him, who with whorish intuition
refrained from modern matriarchy thereby reaping higher
rewards, who made themselves available for the sex urges of
the tycoon and submitted to his attempt to find an inner satis-

faction through sexual contact. Girls who began as models and typists, and who were now snug in fur coats.

But none of these descriptions could be applied to Iole, and the alternative, true love and pure, had naturally already been analyzed, declared unimportant, commercialized and left to ducktails, pop singers, teen-agers, drunk librettists, computers and their cybernetica.

However mysterious it all was, the fact remained that Boris Gudenov was in possession of Iole, and he brought her in his silver gray Rolls-Royce to his flat above the Oita shopping center with its imitation Greek courtyard, marble fountains and bust of Marcus Aurelius — a prison with flowers, a gilded dome, multicolored walls, fruit on the table, thermos flagons, private telephones, music disseminated by PM-4 loudspeakers, bells to summon personal servants, mirrors, shaded lights — the whole sterile complexity with which money serves its master.

He brought her to his "home" where, in other rooms equally luxurious in autumn-colored décor, his wife, Katy, was also waiting for him.

*

Katy, Boris Gudenov's wife, hears about her husband's find and remembers with nostalgia the time when he fought for her hand.

No one knew whether Boris Gudenov had really married Katy; however, she was generally accepted as his lawful wife, and she spent her days in the company of her son Hyllus in the gilded cage on the top floor of the Oita shopping center. Hyllus was a regular little Paul Pry and took great pleasure in keeping his mother supplied with the latest scandal about his father and the girl, Iole. "And he is old enough to be her father," said the young Peeping Tom.

That induced her to think back, as she now so often did, with longing to the past when she was a pretty young girl, the love of Max Aucholos, her young bull of a lover. It was in the little village of Riviersonderend where her parents had lived, and she, the cool silken maiden, with shoulder-length locks, used to pick armfuls of arum lilies in the vlei at dusk. Max there in the reeds with the strength of a bull and the cunning of a snake. And then the appearance of Boris, the up-and-coming young shopkeeper, the darling of all the young women in the neighborhood. The inevitable clash between the two while she looked on, worried but jubilant: the struggle between these two godlike creatures for her cool little hand; the realization that she was desired by two such important figures: the bliss of being desired without having to give anything in return.

She put Hyllus to bed, put out the light and waited for her husband whom she had last seen fifteen months before.

With silent enjoyment she relived her suffering during the years, the days and years of loneliness when her friends commiserated with her — the grass widow waiting patiently for her husband whom she could punish with frigidity when he came . . . (She remembered with resentment his demands, the eternal touching, as though he could turn on her emotions like a tap, as though he had a right to her body, as though her body did not belong to her.)

She was proud of her beauty which, thanks to his wealth, she could pamper with massages, visits to beauty salons, sweet-smelling herbal baths, electromagnetic treatments, professional makeup and all the advantages that beauty culture offered. She sometimes let him see a flesh-colored lace pantie, a sun-bronzed thigh, a flash of her breasts, a nude body just before the door closed on his vulgarity. She knew the mighty Boris Gudenov, and he was not so wonderful. She knew him in all his helplessness when she played frigid and, precisely at the right moment, called his bluff. They said Gudenov was impotent, they said he was a monster — and she always defended him. She quoted him, she referred to him with affectionate teasing, she told stories that sparkled with intimacy and good-natured jesting to demonstrate their special relationship.

She switched on the radio and sank into a chair in front of a large window overlooking the city. She had now reached the second half of her memory cycle, her greatest triumph — the death of Neuman Nessos and Boris Gudenov's jealousy.

Boris Gudenov would always wonder what had happened; it would always gnaw at him. Had they slept together? Had they really committed adultery? Had the whole truth been told about their dear friend, accidentally shot by Boris on safari in the Umfolozi ten years before? She had given him the Hemingway short story, "The Short Happy Life of Francis Macomber," although she knew that Gudenov was an indifferent reader. Whose shadow was silhouetted on the wall of her tent? Why did she still keep the gown on which the bloodstains grew darker each year? It was still hanging in her room, and she unconsciously fingered it when Boris Gudenov spoke to her. She challenged him openly to raise objections. When he explained how the accident had happened, she always remained silent. She did not reproach him; she just looked at him.

The memory cycle was now complete. She began to feel

restless and, rising, walked about the room. She wondered what the new "secretary" looked like, and when there was a knock on the door she opened it herself without bothering to ring for the maid.

Iole greeted her modestly, and Katy instinctively put her hand to her heart.

Dear God, she thought, it could be me, fifteen years ago!

*

Boris Gudenov receives a report from one of his numerous spies that Brigadier Ornassis E. has begun the campaign against him and that a policeman, Demosthenes de Goede, has been appointed to carry out the task. Boris Gudenov finds Demosthenes de Goede very amusing and cannot work up any resentment against him. But he decides that Demosthenes de Goede must be put out of the way and gives instructions to his legion of paid lackeys to that effect..

He knew from bitter experience that one must never underestimate an enemy, that respect for the capabilities of an opponent (someone like Brigadier Ornassis E.) puts you in a position to use those very capabilities indirectly against him (there is a constant dialogue as you are learning to know your enemy). But what do you do when your enemy comes to you naïve, upright and pure in heart? You are immediately disarmed, for no man is so degenerate (or dares admit that measure of degeneracy in himself) as to destroy deliberately what is good. As strange as innocence and virtue were to the tragic concept of Aristotle, just so strange was it to the world of the tycoon whose kingdom was built on the vanity and moral weakness of man.

Demosthenes de Goede had to be destroyed; but before that

could happen, he had to be exposed to the allurements of the
secular world of the tycoon. It was like the struggle between
the matador and the bull in the corrida: the most dangerous
bull was the one that had not been properly bred, that was not
boyante but chose its own ground and did not worry about
the *capa*. Demosthenes de Goede had to reveal a moral weakness, had to be tempted.

It was easier to leave this side of the struggle to underlings.
It was not expected that the tycoon should lower himself to
that extent. The picadors first went to work before the matador began. Boris Gudenov had once appeared in the same
arena as Sidney Franklin and Sir Henry and was immediately
singled out as a Diestro and not a Camelo.

He would first get his lackeys to give Demosthenes de
Goede a workout and perhaps accomplish his destruction without intervening. If the fight had to continue after that, Boris
Gudenov would give it his personal attention — directly and
with finesse as behooved a worthy opponent.

                                 *

*To the question: Who is Boris Gudenov? Brigadier Ornassis
E.'s answer that he was a tycoon is perhaps the only fact that
can be established with any measure of certainty — although by the very nature of the case it is impossible to say
precisely how anyone becomes a tycoon.* *

Although the business world and the stockmarket were based
on a sane, intelligible law like supply and demand, there was
still a legend that certain people were influential enough to

---

* The fact that John Kenneth Galbraith does not mention his name in
his well-known dissertation on the big collapse of 1929 cannot be explained.

transcend that law and, by means of supernatural manipulation in their material world, to determine the future of all interested parties. People like Morgan, Raskob, Sachs, Krueger, Mitchell, Boris Gudenov and others. Such influence is not always bad, but sometimes does good as on that Black Thursday, October 24, 1929, when Morgan and others managed temporarily to stem the selling panic. It often does harm, as in 1928 when Mitchell prevented the Federal Reserve Bank from raising the rate of interest by one percent in time to stop the spiraling of inflation.

It was difficult to determine the role played by Boris Gudenov in this connection. He was a financial genius of scarcely eighteen years and already a legend in an age that lent itself to the birth of legends. He was a young shopkeeper in South Africa. One fine day he turned up in America and immediately saw the possibilities of mergers by means of which giant cartels were formed by controlling companies. That was of course before there were all sorts of awkward laws and at a time when the mad rush of free enterprise gave rise to those colorful pirates on the ocean of financial undertaking.

The assertion was that the principle known as "leverage" was first applied by him when, with a small capital, he established a trust company; and on a basis of one-third debentures, one-third preferentials and one-third ordinary shares, each rise in shares (at a time of easy increase) caused his ordinary shares to treble in value because the debentures and preferential shares naturally remained constant in spite of increased portfolio value. He later discovered that ordinary shares could be made to rise still farther by letting the artificially boosted ordinary shares be taken over by other trust companies which, in their turn, were also based on the "leverage" principle. There was a great demand for ordinary shares, and it could be argued that Boris Gudenov was only supplying a demand. When the Senate committee instituted an investigation into his activities they found nothing wrong with his transactions; but looked at in retrospect, after all the anti-trust laws and laws for the protection of the ordinary share-holders, it could be understood that the image of Boris Gudenov, the creator of that particular system, had become ominous, and that he had gained the reputation of being a Caribbean pirate.

It is common knowledge that after the great crash well known people had disappeared overnight, and a number had committed suicide, but the House of Gudenov had survived. One aspect of this is easily explained: he had pulled out in time. More important: he had withdrawn at a time when the Harvard economists had seen nothing but rose-colored clouds over the financial landscape and had regarded the small black cloud as nothing but the defeatist attitude of a few Leftists. A more difficult side of the question was whether Boris Gudenov had at that time, as opposed to the Morgans and the Rockefellers, a clearer insight into the future, and whether his unobtrusive disappearance (no tycoon dared disappear suddenly without affecting the sensitive market) had been due to an occult rather than a pragmatic power of perception — a realization of the seven lean years following the seven fat years — or had he been warned in time by the first abortive measures against inflation?

Today, in spite of laws which regulated commerce in the finest detail, there were new mergers and new tycoons who were particularly concerned about their image. There were memories of menacing unknowns like Zaharoff. And there were others marking time who had the hound's name — the one with the uncontrollable appetite that was pacified with cake by the Sibyl, the one that was silenced with sand by the magic poet.

According to rumors, Boris Gudenov was egocentric, ruthless, cruel to his enemy (and his friend if he became an enemy), covetous, affectionate but selfish to his family, unsympathetic to his wife, fond of women in general, but short-lived in his affections.

Everyone admitted, however, that he was a remarkable person.

*

Rumors about Boris Gudenov's origin (for the most part possibly apocryphal).

That he came from a *schtetl* in Eastern Europe.

That his great-grandfather was a *Maggid*, blessed with the gift of the third eye.

That his father was one of the thirty-six *Zaddikim* of his time who lived to the glory of God in saintly poverty. The small Boris had had memories of the *tallith* over his father's shoulders. He remembered how, trembling with fear, he had had to open the door when the Angel of Death went by.

As the first generation in a new country such a child often revolts against his background: poverty and the ritual that reminds him of it. He usually finds compensation in the unorthodox, the search for wealth, the striving after power; and he takes delight in the accumulation of knowledge in the cold

world of intellectual power, in the avant-garde adventure of
sharpened insight, in the ruthlessness of selfish love.

He is often a genius.

*

To return to Katy where she last stood, facing Iole.

Deep in her heart she felt sorry for this girl who had lost everything: her father, her brother, her public prestige. She
made an attempt to chat to the lovely child who was trying to
protect herself by remaining silent and, taking her by the hand,
led her through the room. Who could deny it? Indirectly
Iole was responsible for all the disasters that had befallen her
parents' house.

Katy poured tea from a silver pot, and by chance saw herself in the oval looking glass above the table with the lapis
lazuli top. In spite of makeup, her own beauty was becoming harder. Everything about her was a coarse counterfeit of
the natural assets of youth; by imitating, she at once became a
wrinkled hag, and she feared the answer to the question which
she must, in spite of what she knew, put to her mirror.

She turned her back on the glass and directed her attention
to the girl. This was the first time that Boris Gudenov had
brought anyone into the inner circle of their home. It was *her*
sheets that would cover that lovely figure, *her* pillows that
would smother the love cry, *her* bed that would heave on the
wave of love.

And then she changed her plans. She concentrated again on
Gudenov, knowing that nothing would help, that in the complexity of human relations there was no logic. She overcame
the arguments of the plural animus, the ex cathedra wisdom

of the misleading philosophers within herself, and gained a greater victory than she knew.

She would punish him with unselfish love.

*

Boris Gudenov receives Iole in his room, and the battle begins.

She appeared in a Wolsey Vanity Fair nightgown, turquoise blue with pink bows, marabou slippers, a ribbon in her hair and dragon's blood on her lips. He saw her in his luxurious room surrounded by the silken walls, silhouetted against shaded lights, to the accompaniment of music from invisible loudspeakers through the V of two bottles of champagne crossed in the ice bucket. The reputation of the mighty Boris Gudenov was at stake since the bitter affair in Lydia and the mockery that nowadays had more punch than before.

It was the first time that he had been alone with her. He was suitably dressed in a smoking jacket of blue velvet, his hair graying at the temples, apparently in perfect control of the situation and at home in his luxurious surroundings, a picture of manliness, refinement and sophistication, exciting to women because of his appearance of aloofness, fascinating to them because he looked capable of cruelty with the possibility of unexpected tenderness in love: Boris Gudenov who had conquered the world, who at this moment of his vulnerability could hold her in thrall.

He came toward her, took her hands in his and went through all the romantic movements that his invisible judges expected of him. Conquered, she surrendered to him, and the exposure began. But somewhere behind the aloofness was hidden a small boy from the *schtetl* who had had to fetch a kosher chicken for his magical dad, who, trembling with fright, had heard the wings of the Angel of Death rustling in the night; and somewhere there was a little girl who had tasted the loneliness of candlelight and romantic homesickness in an attic room beneath the Swartberg; and there was also the murmur of the sea and the lights of the villa on the Côte d'Azur with its lure of a strange decadence; and somewhere something important had gone hopelessly wrong, and something burst with the fierceness of a magnesium flare in confined spaces, spreading fireworks in a dark night of absolute isolation. There was a diamond-hard central core which followed everything with cold eyes, and there was a childlike desire that nothing physical should take place, but that on the wings of sleep Boris Gudenov should be great and strong like the prince of love, and that she should receive him like the princess of desire in the pleasure garden of their dreams.

They were going through the movements on the blade-thin dividing line between salvation and ruin, when the red telephone rang and the moment was lost.

And Boris Gudenov learned that Demosthenes de Goede, shod with loafers, had just begun his campaign.

THE WAY TO THE
SHOPPING CENTER

Suburbia · Captain Demosthenes de
Goede, dressed like one of the Stray
Satan gang, in leather jacket, stove pipe pants
and loafers, denuded of his Beretta, but formidable
enough on account of his powerful physique, was on his
way to the center of the city and the Oita shopping center
where he had a task to perform about which he was not at all
clear. But like all practical people he overcame problems by
oversimplification, reduced compounds to basic facts, submitted to the single, established data which would couple life's
theorem to an irrefutable conclusion.

The human psyche was as much an enigma to him as the
concept of eternity; his knowledge of man was based on for-
mulae and character sketches that he had learned in the police
college and from literature, and on behavior patterns that he
had observed in life when a given character had reacted to a
given situation according to the textbook. In the end, how did
one know oneself and one's fellowmen? How could the ordinary man enter that world of the unconscious, how could he
break through the barrier of nothing?

His task was simple: he had to find out everything about
Boris Gudenov; he had to examine the scene of abstract crime
and note down every scrap of concrete evidence.

*

The side streets of the suburb leading to the city through
semi-detached houses like his own were so alike that you could
easily go astray if you were not an habitué. It was already
quite dark, and the shadows of the occupants were thrown
against the colored window curtains. Each open window re-

vealed chrome chairs next to a brick fireplace, giving a uniform picture into the lives of the invisible people behind other open windows. Nothing moved; his footsteps resounded loudly on the concrete; every corner of the small gardens, all alike, was silent and empty. Then unexpectedly a figure loomed up, still and motionless — an eternal gnome cast in concrete above a fish pond.

Around the corner, Captain Demosthenes de Goede suddenly saw someone like himself approaching under a streetlamp: a tall gangling fellow with a purposeful shuffle and a ducktail hairdo, a strong chin and quarrelsome eyes — a teenager whose face expressed touchiness. They approached each other slowly with their hands in their pockets clenching a jackknife and an imaginary Beretta.

They came cautiously, looking each other straight in the eyes: checkmate. Then they passed on: Demosthenes de Goede with enormous arms and a leather jacket straining against his shoulder muscles; the stranger with sectarian comfort written across his broad shoulders: "Jesus Saves!"

It seemed that the little streets had no end, streets that never wavered but formed, nevertheless, a labyrinth of right angles. The Captain walked on relentlessly, around a block, and then under a corner streetlight his way was suddenly blocked by a girl with a mane like a wolf — mousy, stringy hair, puffed up with the help of cheap hairspray — towering above black eyelids and corpse-white lips, all adding up to the teen-age idea of redemption. He wanted to pass her by and pretended not to notice her suggestive movements. Always ready to accept the challenge of any woman, he steeled himself against his inclinations, but she stepped in front of him and said: "Come on,

honey . . ." Captain Demosthenes de Goede found this first
obstacle in the path of his duty tiresome; not because he found
her irresistible, but because she symbolized that desire for
chaos that was in him, that wish to be free. She smiled suddenly as though she realized the clash of purpose in his nature
and was mocking him. He pushed her aside, turned down the
next side street and found himself hopelessly lost in surroundings that should have been familiar to him.

The streets became darker and the buildings, so nondescript
by day, suddenly seemed menacing. The mighty Captain de
Goede, who did not know fear, now experienced another kind
of fear: a longing for his wife and children, a feeling that he
would never see them again, that the home to which he had
always returned in the past in some mysterious way did not
exist any longer, and that he would be alone for the rest of his
life. He tried to shake off the presentiment, walking faster,
turning back down the street, always to the left like all lost
people. Then he heard her voice again, close to him in the
darkness, "Come on, honey . . ." and he caught a glimpse of
her wolf hair which, for a moment, gleamed like phosphorus
under the streetlamp.

Demosthenes de Goede stopped, squared his shoulders and
shook off his fear. He thought of Hope and her words of en-
couragement after the party when he had had doubts about
his mission. She had explained away all his objections: it was
the climax of his career, this adventure into a new sphere, this
great undertaking which rose above the banality of his previous tasks. Hope had taught him to be unselfish, his Viking
wife who was prepared to accept loneliness for the sake of
this higher call upon him.

Captain Demosthenes de Goede pulled himself together, and with renewed direction of purpose wandered about the suburb with firm steps, thinking of his lovely wife. Around every corner came the mocking challenge, "Honey, it's good . . ." but he was deaf to her voice and blind to her animal nature.

When even the tireless Captain began to feel worn out, and his footsteps were no longer so firm, he met the ducktail again on his around-the-block beat and went forward threateningly to meet him. Brusquely he asked him the way to the city. He was examined by two green eyes from which shone the light of obsession, and he received a sermon from one who had found salvation.

"I was like you," said the reformed ducktail happily. "I also slept with whores and worshiped the god of alcohol. I also looked in vain for the truth, and in my utmost misery I saw the light."

They were walking together now, these two in leather jackets and loafers.

"I smoked dagga and puked on the temple of God."

He indicated a street to the left and one to the right. The houses looked alike, the streets were dark and far removed from the city lights.

"I can dance the Letkajenka, the Watusi, the Surf, the Frug and the Swim," said the dedicated ducktail proudly. "I saw Abaddon and returned."

"I think it's to the left," he said at the next corner.

"I got drunk on kosher wine," he said as they entered another dark street and looked in vain at the glass windows with the rainbow-colored curtains.

"I devoted myself to radical Christian ethics," said the

transfigured ducktail when they came to the following corner. "Christ would have understood the secularization of our times; he would have laughed at the mystery that the old people were so mad over and that drives us to drink and evil." His green eyes were fixed on the Captain as they turned to the left under a streetlight and moved forward laboriously. "He stands by Youth. He belongs to this world. Demonology has clay feet. He speaks a new language. His language is not about angels and devils but about housing, the franchise and living space." The ducktail paused suddenly, exhausted. "Have you got somewhere to sleep?"

Captain Demosthenes de Goede explained that he only wanted to find the city.

The ducktail of Christ pointed to a bus disappearing around the corner. "Why don't you take a bus?" he asked.

*

Transport.

Only when Demosthenes de Goede was on the thundering bus closely packed with people hardly two inches apart, isolated in the desert of their own existence, looking straight ahead with discouraged eyes, their faces stark with the sobering realization of something trying to penetrate their confused thoughts, their bodies tensed by an indecision that pinned them to their seats — only when Demosthenes de Goede had become one of them, and, like the rest, saw the conductor coming down the aisle and looked at his clicking clippers, the different colored tickets, his swaying motion following the rhythm of the bus — only when the figure of A. C. Theron in his municipal khaki jacket, his sleeves bound with leather, his hair long and his shirt collar frayed, his eyes yellow and sick of the same faces, the same routes, and the same memories, stood before him — only when the yellow, gold-filled teeth were bared in a grimace at this tardiness in paying and the dirty nails tapped impatiently against the silver clippers and the nicotine stained thumb riffled through the tickets — only when the hollow cheeks flushed angrily and the fever red lips became a thin line at the unpleasant presentiment of "more trouble" — only then did Captain Demosthenes de Goede realize that the dedicated ducktail had relieved him of all his cash.

Captain Demosthenes de Goede explained slowly that he would pay back the amount (seven and a half cents) later, but the conductor's professional dignity was at stake. He rang the bell and the bus came to a standstill. Such irregularity he could not countenance. The citizen *manes*, sitting in regimented pairs, lost their characteristic expression of apathy and looked hopefully at the situation boiling up which would provide an exciting topic of conversation and speculation for the next few days.

The Captain and the conductor looked at each other in their different uniforms, and each waited for the other to take the next step which would decide matters one way or another. Municipal authority was binding in the long run, but there were early stages when the poor official had to depend on himself to cope with an uncertain future.

Then the conductor, having looked in vain to the other passengers, tried reeling off a string of swear words — impressive, but irrelevant. When that did not help, he stammered out the relevant regulations and referred vaguely to sanctions that he did not understand properly. Then, at his wits' end, he presented himself as a champion for the city council. He grabbed Demosthenes de Goede by his arm to pull him out of his seat and received a blow that sent him staggering the length of the bus. He rose slowly and without dignity. Ringing the bell for the bus to proceed, he shouted threats from a safe distance, knowing that time would bring revenge and that all the powers of the city administration would in the end be on his side.

When the bus stopped in the middle of the town and the passengers all disappeared quickly, impelled by whatever urge it was that drove them on, the conductor wondered if it would be worth all the trouble for seven and a half cents.

He came to a decision and rang the bell. The bus thundered on accompanied by the clanging, and the conductor found a peculiar reassurance in the noise. Each docile new passenger who obeyed his orders added salve to his wounds; each response of the diesel motor to his bell pushed the unpleasant memory a little farther away, and he was soon again part of the orderliness that did not brook any liberties. He seemed to give his instructions and click his clippers with greater abandon, to pull out the tickets more smartly and hand them over more threateningly. He had been free for a space, and it was enough to make him appreciate his lack of freedom.

*

The shopping center.

Captain Demosthenes de Goede stood in the center of the city in front of the shopping center, surrounded by people moving to and fro in the fog — a fog that rolled over the vast table-like mountain and threw a shadow over the city and the sea, increasing in the night until it became the gaping maw of Lion's Head, gnawing at the earth with fangs of cloud. The electric lights were polarized by the mirrors of the shopping center; the moonlight shimmered faintly at one point through the curtain of mist — an alchemistic light like the glimmer of a dying day and an awakening night. Under its surface of tar the Heerengracht snaked its way to the sea, a stream of many memories that carried one's thoughts to oblivion, disappearing unsorted through pitch-black pipes into the bosom of the ocean. A single ambulance screamed its way like a vulture through the streets; foghorns, like owls, hooted their presentiment of approaching disaster; yew trees, imprisoned in railings along the sides of the streets, dreamed their restless dreams in company with the few sleepers. Gudenov's palace was right in the middle of the town. It was brightly lit by a myriad of lights, but the dark patches, where the lights could not reach, were darker than the darkest places in the town.

Captain Demosthenes de Goede was jostled from all sides by the crowds on the sidewalk, but he was too proud to lift a finger. He looked at the weak, negative faces and the double stream moving in opposite directions, and they seemed to be blown by the whims of the wind which came tearing down the street tunnels from all sides. He waylaid a passing paterfamilias and asked him if he knew anything about Boris Gudenov.

The man stopped uncertainly and looked at the vigorous figure in the leather jacket. Somewhat embarrassed, he looked around nervously and found a measure of security in the crowds about him. He decided that the ever-present dangerous situation did not in this case constitute a personal threat to him. Perhaps this was an artist, a representative of the Cape Performing Arts Board, who was promoting a show.

"Boris Gudenov is a ballet dancer," he said cautiously.

Captain Demosthenes de Goede wrote down this information in his pocket notebook. The man reconsidered his first impression: perhaps this was someone from the Bureau of Consumer Statistics.

"It's a deodorant," said the man. "It comes in a plastic bottle with a roll-on cap."

Captain Demosthenes de Goede wrote it down.

"Boris Gudenov is a writer who won the Nobel Prize," said the man in despair.

He gave his name and address somewhere in Vredehoek and disappeared in consternation in the opposite direction from which he had come.

Captain Demosthenes de Goede looked at the townspeople searchingly and with suspicion. He saw how they scuttled back and forth as if something were driving them on; he was a solid object in the stream, spying on the world. It was a new experience for him to make such general observations, and it was the first time in his life that he was not committed to the solution of a specific crime. He thought it was all a wild-goose chase — as though that was an original thought. He enlarged on this and saw something of himself in everyone: the pattern of his life woven into the larger pattern of continual change. Life is so short, he thought. As a youngster he had told himself: I want to be a king. I want to liberate mankind. I want to win women's hearts. I want to be a pope. I want to be a general on the field of battle. I want to visit foreign places and overcome the lotus existence on tropical islands. There is something that drives me like the wind. House — palace — hut in the prune stones on my plate. Time is running out, time is running out . . . He listened to the music behind the glass doors of the shopping center; he looked up and saw the Gudenov slogan above the entrance; he stood among the crowds — a huge man, undecided and full of memories, a magnificent creature with a kind heart, ready to serve.

Someone tapped him on the elbow, and the dedicated duck-tail's face peeped over his shoulder.

"I've brought your money back," he said. "It was force of habit, but I've won the battle." He shivered and shook in time to the music issuing from the building, and he pressed the notes into the large hand. "Why don't you go inside?" He boomps-boompsed from side to side and shook his shoulders in double time while his feet moved at lightning speed. Then he stopped suddenly.

"What is your wife's name?" asked the converted ducktail, still keeping time lightly with his loafers. He looked at the giant and gave him a playful blow in the stomach.

"Hope," said Captain Demosthenes de Goede, and he thought suddenly of all the young boys that he had, in his police career, brought before the sergeant's desk from the back streets.

The ducktail smiled.

"You have to keep up with the times," he said. "You must know the rhythm: the shivers and shakes of our age." He embraced Demosthenes de Goede, and the latter's face assumed a good-natured expression. "Get with it!" yelled the ducktail as a wave of music hit them. He controlled himself immediately. His self-discipline was now evident in the absence of rhythmic movement. He became limp and womanly in his submission when it reached his thought level. He pushed his thin wiry arm through the Captain's substantial one and led him unnoticed to the door of the shopping center.

"One must try to distinguish between reason and mystic revelation," said the transfigured ducktail. "We live in this world, don't we?" He looked at the Captain with youthful green eyes under long lashes. "Order and religion are based on this world; revelation is directed to this earth, isn't that so?" He pressed his wiry body against the sturdy one of Captain Demosthenes de Goede. "The secular order is the order of the new Christ, isn't it?" He peered cautiously at Captain Demosthenes de Goede who did not understand a word, and was beginning to wriggle out of the embrace.

"Hope is a whore," said the offended ducktail suddenly, and dodged like lightning as a powerful punch cleft a hole in the air in the direction of the text on his back.

*

Captain Demosthenes de Goede entered the hall of the shopping center through which a stream of people moved deliberately, and also, in a way, involuntarily. They seemed to hate the place with its unashamed exploitation, but could not do without it; as though the sort of life which was their lot with its hurry and inconstant values roused a fear of, as well as an incomprehensible necessity for, participation. The Oita of Boris Gudenov, with everything from a needle to an anchor, had, like all institutions born of their own necessity, become a symbol of the decadent mode of life that everyone criticized but no one rejected. There was not one who entered the gate who did not hate the twentieth-century organization: the collective sterile narcissism, the unrequested product that was palmed off by means of psychological persuasion, the condoned dissipation that roused loathing, the way of life that bred anxiety, all the things that you feared but still desired. They were like cuckolds compelled by the complexity of the social structure to be the confidants of their wives' fellow transgressors; like abandoned wives who desired their husbands' mistresses, Lesbian fashion. Their degenerate will was the creator of these degenerate times. They were co-architects of Boris Gudenov's shopping centers everywhere in the world.

Captain Demosthenes de Goede entered the shopping center cautiously and found the reassuring banality of every day: there were floors below and floors above; strings of tinsel festooned in circles among gold papier-mâché decorations; escalators easing the way to the gay well of merchandise; and always music — a discordant cacophony of schmaltz, light opera, pop ballads, hillbilly tunes, atonal jazz, mood music and folk songs — being pounded layer by layer into everyone's head.

It was an orchestra of dissonance and Captain Demosthenes de Goede immediately felt at home. Here he would get the hound Gudenov.

*

The code.

Brigadier Ornassis E. lay on the triple bed in his flat and looked worriedly at Hope restoring her hair and her face in front of the mirror. He saw her from behind and noticed all the marks on her back, the shoulder straps of her petticoat that were too tight and left red stripes after each movement, the arms that had looked so soft and now appeared muscular, the hair that seemed primitive from neglect before combing and fashionably primitive after punishment with a comb. He took note of her small waist, her relaxed thigh muscles and the breasts enlarged to mountains by snow white falsies. For some inexplicable reason he began to long for the lithe young men of the D-Service.

He was busy reading to her from a communication on government service paper.

"Boris Gudenov is a ballet dancer," he read. "Boris Gudenov is a deodorant. Boris Gudenov won the Nobel Prize."

The screams of the De Goede children, locked in the room next door, interrupted his words. He waited until a blood-curdling yell prefaced the next silence.

"It's a remarkable code," he said.

Hope turned and came toward him temptingly, dressed only in her petticoat, her legs longer than usual because of her high Italian spike heels. The Brigadier forced himself not to look at her and studied the interesting code attentively. He felt her sitting next to him on the bed and smelled her exotic perfume. As she had repeatedly done in the past, she offered her services in the battle against Boris Gudenov. She was sure that she could do her part as a woman in this matter.

The Brigadier considered the situation carefully while he stared blindly at the document in his hand which had begun to tremble slightly. As he had had to do so many times in his life, he had to make a decision. He suddenly decided in the affirmative, and when she expressed her gratitude in the only way she knew, he realized too late that his timing was faulty.

*

Some time later in the day the Brigadier, surrounded by his brilliant young men, waited in the gymnasium of the D-Service for the code to be deciphered by the personnel group. He looked particularly smart in a Harris tweed jacket with a matching silk scarf around his neck. The circles under his eyes lent a certain dignity to his striking appearance; his nervous movements displayed that interesting tension so characteristic of him when he was demanding the highest efficiency from his staff.

"Boris Gudenov is a ballet dancer," repeated a member of the personnel group while the young men of the action front formed a pyramid and maintained the construction with trembling muscles. He looked at a couple of notes that he had jotted down on paper, and continued. "We all know the effeminate qualities of ballet dancers. Have we perhaps to do with an archetypal image of the anima?"

The Brigadier waited patiently until the excited exchange of words had calmed down and motioned without comment to another young man, while the pyramid collapsed and the action front turned somersaults and landed lightly on their feet.

"Boris Gudenov is a deodorant," read the young man. "Perhaps a reference to the magic talisman? Something like the *ephialtion?*"

The Brigadier, lost in thought, looked at the action front who were jumping up on one another's shoulders and slowly building up a human monolith. He waited until the last man, with a mighty leap, reached the top level, and then nodded to the third young man from the personnel division. "Boris Gudenov is a Nobel Prize winner. It's obviously an attempt by Captain de Goede to test our credulity. It's a word play on Boris Pasternak."

The totem pole waved from side to side while a further argument followed as to whether that was true to the nature of one like Demosthenes de Goede, but the brilliant young man defended his viewpoint heatedly; in his opinion simple people were especially capable of reaching a height of subtlety in satire which was not commensurate with their intellectual powers — witness the efficacy of their social commentary by means of scatological jokes. The knees of the lowest member of the totem gave way, and the whole bunch collapsed like a house of cards. The Brigadier listened attentively to the argument that followed, and looked at the member of the action front who was carried away on a stretcher. He allowed his young men to discuss the code further while the action group catapulted one another through the air from a springboard. Now and then he took part in the discussion without airing his opinion. Toward the end of the interview he went and stood on the springboard himself and was sent through the air with a mighty sweep. The young men looked at their Brigadier with respect as he flew through the air and ended the argument when he was neatly caught by a member of the action front. After that the meeting was adjourned.

The Brigadier was very relieved when he returned to his tastefully furnished room and found that Hope had already left. She had thoughtfully made him some ham sandwiches and had remembered to be lavish with the mustard. Although she had tidied the room, there were signs everywhere of her presence there the night before: a forgotten handkerchief, tissues in the wastepaper basket, cologne in the bathroom, a floral head scarf of pure nylon and, on the table next to his bed where she had obviously forgotten it, a small bottle of some unfamiliar liquid.

Brigadier Ornassis E. sniffed at it and tried to analyze its contents, but that would have been difficult for anyone not conversant with ingredients like miura, puama, lecithin, aronacein and others.

He went to the room next door where the De Goede children had slept on the floor, surrounded by all sorts of games like snakes and ladders, draughts, Chinese checkers and Happy Families. The state of the room was indescribable, and he sincerely pitied Hope: the mother who had to devote her life, day after day, to the young; the tyranny of children who made selfish demands and wore down her creative urge with their never-ending urge to live. Leave them alone for a moment, and they would destroy themselves. That was the tragedy of life, he thought as he went back and poured himself a drink, that children during their dependent years sapped the life of their mothers.

After a couple of drinks he felt cheerful and even ready to forgive the children. Then the doorbell rang and Hope appeared at the front door: a striking image of Woman, in gold, generously endowed beyond the powers of description, surrounded by her tattered children who each made a timely snatch at a ham sandwich before they disappeared with instinctive discipline, like homing pigeons, to the room where snakes and ladders and cards were waiting.

The Brigadier, a man of worldly wisdom, was aware that he was burning the candle at both ends. But he was also aware of the demands of our times on the Service. He was tired, but upright and ready to accept the challenge. He looked at

Hope's hot blue eyes fixed on him, and he saw how she had loosened her hair about her shoulders, and how she was taking the customary few steps of a pre-orgastic dance to music that welled up from a deep erotic source and charged her whole being with a life-giving passion that made her radiate with sparkling energy, as if the rising sun was burning inside her.

The heroic struggle often takes place unseen, and in unusual places; and just as on the battlefield, it deserves its troubadours — those specialists in illusion, those winged liars of all time.

*

Limbo.

Boris Gudenov's thoughts, in a flight of reverie, formed a cloud over the cold kernel of his reason. He sat alone at the window of his room while the girl slept. According to legend, he did not know the ecstacy of absolute faith, because his destiny was a particular torment: he was a square peg in a round hole; a hero in an unheroic age, a genius, a throwback; and he stood alone in the pure, almost classic, perfection of his world. They said he was like the sun, that destroyed everything that approached too closely, but caused everything at a distance to grow. He could only achieve his salvation by destruction caused by a woman.

He looked at the girl, sleeping so peacefully, in the knowledge that he could never torture her with true love. He was Boris Gudenov, and Boris Gudenov was impotent, with the impotence of pure reason — the sexless product of the unchained spirit.

*

The wailing women.

"I feel sorry for her," said Katy, crossing her shapely legs and nodding to the maid to serve the champagne and snacks. "I pity her," she repeated to the women of her bridge club who were tasting the snacks and gossiping spitefully, interested in one another's husbands, and in their forties, temporarily winning the battle against age with the help of cosmetics and diet.

"I can see my own bitter life lying ahead of the poor child," she said, sucking in her cheeks to make the attractive hollows permanent.

A chorus of beautiful, sophisticated women sang their praises of the loving nature of their dear hostess and they speculated about the irony of fate, while they washed down caviar sandwiches with champagne. They bewailed the lot of their large-eyed hostess: the lonely wife in her gilded cage, the arch of solitary nights over the bed of Paradise, the wandering loneliness that tormented her in the empty house. It was a sympathetic chorus of friends, all cold ghosts of former brides who, adulterous in thought and coquettish in deed, wanted to exorcise loneliness from their own middle age.

They consumed the least number of calories in the most pleasant form for the sake of slender hips, and faultlessly decried the fate of their friend who was burdened by lustiness, without an object to love, in tune with the universal discontent of all women, their own organs of love bronze shields in the battle of sexual assertions.

*

A warning from the Mezeritzer.

If in doubt, turn to the right.

If you see a young woman in the arms of an old man, murder follows.

Boris Gudenov looked at Iole, who awoke, opened her eyes and smiled at him.

Sir Henry believed that you could regain strength through young women; that you could regain youth through strong young women.

But Gudenov's mamma wept real tears in the *schtetl* when she lit the candles on Sabbath evenings.

*

Pallas Athene.

Captain Demosthenes de Goede's ears became accustomed with difficulty to the groove music that was piped to all floors from a sound pit in the basement. It was a ballad of teen-age yearning to the accompaniment of electronic guitars, interpreted by manic-depressive *castrati*.

"It's the sonic limit," said the dedicated ducktail, anaesthetized by the pulsating rhythm.

Even if the Captain battered him flat, he would be attacking an empty shell. The wiry ducktail had a girl on his arm who wriggled lightly with him in time to the beat.

"This is Minie," he said, pushing the girl forward.

She looked at him dully with brown eyes that nevertheless sparkled like polished ebony. The beehive on her head glittered with gold threads; the wings of imaginary bees moving at lightning speed in imaginary flights of thought. She smiled, showing strong white teeth, and licked her lips with her tongue until they shone. She was propelled by a further bump, and said, "Boris Gudenov is sick."

BEE-BEE-DOO

Bee-Bee-Doo · Captain Demosthenes H. de Goede accepted as his lot that
he had to endure the company of teen-agers
and descended the escalator with them under the
swaying, flimsy decorations — the Queen of Sheba and
her train of followers on the way to see Solomon, floating
dolls suspended on silver wires from the dome of the shopping center. A number of clients were frozen in various atti-
tudes on the escalator: some with one foot on the next step,
some stiff and straight, others with their head cocked to the
golden dome. A floorwalker, dressed in black and accoutered
in a snow white collar, ran an expert eye over them as they
landed with a jerk on terra firma and recovered their equilib-
rium among the crowd.

They were surrounded by the charivari of this particular
floor: record bars, discotheques, tearooms, bargain counters
and photo studios. From one of the stalls came the voice of
Dylan Thomas reading from *Adventures in the Skin Trade*,
directed by a teen-ager behind a counter; from other cubicles
came the voice and melody of the day, as determined by public
vote and interpreted by the electronic brain of the computer.
On the wall there were life-size photographs of Marilyn Mon-
roe, Gina Lollobrigida, Jean Harlow, Kim Novak and others.
As far as they could see above the faces of the citizenry
stretched a photographic panorama of feminine beauty, an
enraptured procession apparently in thrall to Eros, the father-
mother of all higher consciousness.

A smallish man, dressed in a white jacket, who had been
watching the scene from a table in the corner, tapped on the
wood with his baton when he saw that the numbers had

grown large enough to warrant his attention. The noise sub-
sided and everyone crowded inquisitively about the man with
the shaggy eyebrows who was blowing his nose, clearing his
throat and drawing in his breath, letting it whistle through his
teeth, as a warming-up exercise before beginning his speech.
He first dealt quickly with a couple of advertisements, then
welcomed them all on behalf of the shopping center and introduced himself as the Man Who Knows — the one with his
ear tuned in to Hollywood and Vine. He pointed with his
baton and had something to say about each portrait as he
moved down the line, followed by the crowds — a bit about
Jean, Gina and Joan; scraps of scandal, and the names of the
films in which they had appeared, while the girl at the records
supplied suitable background music. Then he planted himself
in front of the biggest portrait of all and, holding his pointer
four inches away from two enormous blue eyes, he uttered a
single name: Bee-Bee-Doo!

There was an immediate response: they all knew her, the
Filia Mystica. They remembered all the films they had seen
of her and listened tensely to the tragedy that repeated itself
every decade: the tragedy of Jean Harlow, Marilyn, Clara
Bow and all the others — a tragedy that reached its peak in
the life of Bee-Bee-Doo.

The little man dealt with her early years with dispatch. She
was born thirty years before, to needy parents. When she was
a child, her stepfather often beat her, and then comforted her
with caresses which led, in her thirteenth year, to incest which
she first regarded as normal, but later, when she was grown
up, as an unforgivable crime. She went through the usual
madness of a teen-age marriage and was divorced a year later.
She failed sixth grade. Her name was Luna Cohen, and she

was a lonely child, an ugly duckling who would one day emerge as a swan. She first worked as a nude model in Hollywood, under the impression that they were taking art photographs of her. She played small parts as an actress for a company making documentary films. Driven by hunger, she became the mistress of a publicity agent, and in consequence was given better parts. An enterprising young producer made her a star in a Biblical drama, and won fame for them both. After that she earned thirty thousand rand a week.

The little man paused for a moment and looked at the children eating ice cream, and at their parents staring with unchaste thoughts at the portrait of Bee-Bee-Doo. He eased his collar with his forefinger and rested his larynx; he wiped the perspiration from his forehead with a floral handkerchief. He looked small, slight and ugly below Bee-Bee-Doo who was enthroned above him, in all her glory.

She had been married five times: to a writer, an artist, a musician, an athlete and a millionaire, but each marriage had been a failure. They were all older men, and yet she had not found the security that she had searched for so assiduously. She became world famous and won five Oscars, but Bee-Bee-Doo was deeply unhappy. She liked parties, fast cars, reading, music, dancing, riding, swimming, green bedrooms and Persian rugs. She slept naked, and the whole world spied on her with cameras. And yet Bee-Bee-Doo was lonely and often wept over sorrows that were difficult to explain. She was constantly ill and had had trouble with her wisdom teeth. One day she was found dead, a naked goddess, lifeless against a background of apple green. The whole world mourned, and everyone wanted to now why she had indirectly taken her own life.

The little man felt in his pocket and took out a crumpled scrap of paper from which he began to read with difficulty as soon as he had put on his old-fashioned gold-rimmed spectacles.

"Writers wrote about Bee-Bee-Doo," he read laboriously. "A Dutch poet burst into tears when he heard of her death. Everyone asked for the real reason for her death, and they agreed that we were all to blame." He looked up from the paper, peering over his lenses at the children who had finished eating their ice cream and were now trying to stay their unappeasable appetites with spun sugar. "It is we, the public, and all the organizations that exploited her as a commercial product and ignored the human being behind the merchandise," he continued, "but we can go further than that. We can put the question: Who was Bee-Bee-Doo? Was she a temptress, a whore, an angel of Satan — or was she a beacon, a symbol of love, profane as well as divine?" He took off his glasses, wiped the lenses, tested them against the light and, replacing them, returned to his abstruse script which he began to attack all over again. "Eros belongs to the universe," he read. "The one who creates for man has little control over his or her life and becomes the victim of his or her daemon. You examine yourself and become aware of an inner, endless, mysterious significance. The candlelight flickers, and life becomes impersonal — a burning confluence that you, in your human weakness, cannot tolerate. There is something stretching from heaven right down into the depths of hell." His voice became fiery, involuntarily inflamed by the significance of words that he could sense but not understand. "She had seen enough. She had heard the laughter; she had seen the

clown on the stage and shared in the absurdity. With her eyes
open she had admitted the presence of the unknown, and she
had gone forward into the demoniac as well as the good, into
that something that could lead one to madness and yet transport one into the heights of ecstasy. She had to accept the risk
of her knowledge and had crashed through fear. She was the
Akhamôth that spiraled like a whirlwind in darkness and emp-
tiness in search of the light which she had seen and lost. She
was the fallen Sophia who could not attain the Pleroma; she
was the Holy Ghost of the Earth who could not, without
mediation, go farther than the Horos."

The little man folded the paper slowly and waited a short
while for the background music to reach the required mood.
Meanwhile he looked at the teen-agers who were sedately
putting up with his speech for the sake of the music, and at
their parents who put up with anything for the sake of their
children. In the incomprehensible world in the shadow of the
mushroom cloud, anything went; in the blast, purpose was
united with wisdom; the glow that came from the bright pillar
illuminated a new alliance. In the meantime they waited patiently until they understood what was at stake, just like Captain Demosthenes de Goede who made careful notes and let
his muscles relax until such time as he would be expected to
do something dynamic.

The little man seemed much happier. The first stage was
past, and the next part he knew by heart. He even allowed
himself the liberty of embroidering a little, as his own con-
tribution to her death.

He was telling them about the interment of Bee-Bee-Doo.
"She lay in state at Forest Lawns in the Dylan Thomas room,

under a portrait of the poet who died of insult to the brain. She was dressed in white and was laid out on an apple green ottoman. The service was held in the chapel of the Ecumenical Church of Enlightened Protestants. The coffin cost fifteen thousand rand, and was made of silver and bronze washed with green to suggest oxidation and corruption — the destiny of us all. The Beatles sang "A Hard Day's Night," and the Animals "Hallelujah I Love Her So."

He now had their undivided attention, and made full use of the opportunity. "In the Artists' Plot in Forest Lawns, she lies in her grave under a simple black gravestone, designed by Alan Marshall, the creator of the Flamenco 7, the Raven and all those sports cars she loved so much — his final tribute, in tangible form, to a sublime body by God."

The music became louder and louder and suddenly a voice filled the hall — a pure, agonizing sound, strengthened by 250-watt amplifiers to almost unbearable stereophonic precision. It was the voice of Bee-Bee-Doo and the song that had made her famous.

The little man had stopped talking and looked at his audience who were unconsciously anticipating every note and modulation. And then the teen-agers took over: they had gotten rid of all the candy, and their supple bodies automatically began to pay a last tribute by performing the steps of the Frug. Bee-Bee-Doo was not dead. Even at her grave, there were loudspeakers built into the headstone which teen-age pilgrims set going by putting five cents into the slot to hear her voice again over Forest Lawns and to indulge in black magic of their necromancy among the graves, and to satisfy their craving for the wisdom of the dead.

Minie and the dedicated ducktail were well to the fore: she, more sedate in her alliance with the goddess of light; he, like quicksilver in his movement, the Hermes of the shopping center. When the last note died away and everyone came to a standstill, the little man made a final announcement. There were photographs of film stars, taken at the bier of Bee-Bee-Doo, available at fifteen cents each. They could be found at counter number four. Then he withdrew from the proceedings and retired to his corner, where he changed his white coat for his sports jacket. Out of a tin lunch box he took some sandwiches, which he would have to eat in a hurry to be ready for the next show.

Captain Demosthenes de Goede bought a picture of James Dean at the bier of Bee-Bee-Doo and walked over to the little man who was now drinking tea. He found him an indifferent conversationalist and extremely aggressive.

Captain Demosthenes de Goede wanted to know if he had any knowledge of Boris Gudenov.

"He's my employer," said the little man between gulps of weak, sweet tea.

With difficulty Demosthenes de Goede controlled his temper.

He asked whether he could give him any *information* about Boris Gudenov.

The little man wiped his chin, folded his handkerchief and looked calculatingly at Demosthenes de Goede. He glanced furtively all around, and beckoned. With his hand in the inner pocket of his jacket, he said, "For five rand I'll give you a photo of Boris Gudenov and Bee-Bee-Doo."

Demosthenes de Goede paid the five rand and saw the familiar face of a man, neatly dressed in black, erect, stern and aloof, next to an ottoman on which a girl lay stretched, illuminated by seven candles, her face drained of color by death, but garishly restored to artificial life by the art of the cosmetic department of Haven & Heller, the friendly embalmers.

*

Code number two.

The brilliant young men of Brigadier Ornassis E. were undergoing the usual aptitude tests of the D-Service scheme. Each young man was sunk in concentration, trying to establish the significance-pattern of the questioner before answering the questions.

The questions were simple.

"Are you in love with your father or your mother?"

"Is Boganski, the wrestler, a greater figure in his sphere than e e cummings, the poet, in his?"

"In your leisure time, do you prefer a book or a trowel?"

"Do you find an unattractive woman more intresting than an intelligent man?"

Brigadier Ornassis E. summarily interrupted the test when he read Captain Demosthenes de Goede's notes which a messenger had handed to him. He found it very effective to break into their set schedule with an unexpected problem.

"A communication from Captain de Goede," he said. "Bee-Bee-Doo is the fallen Akhamôth." He waited a moment. "Any comments?"

One of his young men made a cautious attempt.

"In that case, one can regard Bee-Bee-Doo as a Barbelô. Is she a Prounikos? Is it her task to deprive the Archons of the light of the spiritual seed through lust?"

Another expanded on this. "Is she the one who through the

ages moves from one body to another by metempsychosis and summons everyone to the earth and the dissemination of the seed?"

Another saw a relationship between her and Hope. He asked, "Is she the mother of incantation and love philters?"

A fourth wanted to know: "Is she the anima figure that becomes united with the Great Silence; is she the culmination of opposites, the chance wisdom that is also wisdom in intention?"

But the Brigadier had already read out the following communication: "Hope is a whore." His words came in clear and measured tones, and the young men looked at him cautiously and speechlessly.

Then one from the action front ventured an answer. "Perhaps that is Captain de Goede's famous — even notorious — ironic style." He hesitated a moment. "Hope to be a whore — that is the final irony in the Gudenov world — Beatrice becoming banal, emotion becoming counterfeit, the sin of the Wolf."

The Brigadier smiled at the young men of the personnel group who were excitedly urging one another on to contradict the Philistine. He lit a cigarette and blew the smoke up toward the gilded roof.

"Of course we all realize that Captain de Goede has only just begun his journey," he said softly. He was particularly friendly, and made the hasty young man from the action front feel small by his forgiving disposition. He turned toward the young man of the personnel group who had spoken earlier. "I think in this case we should rather think of the image of Dositheus' Helena, and of Simon Magus' universal mother prostitute." The young man smiled happily. "Love philters and incantations," mused the Brigadier, "ought to give us a lead."

One of the other young men wanted to cap this line of thought by suggesting the Brigadier himself as someone like Simon Magus, the upright man, the one who imagined he had the face of Zeus, but he thought better of it in time.

"If Beatrice, in the words of the great poet, becomes Sophia," continued the Brigadier, "then Hope can become Selene or Helen — the Light, the product of inspiration and eternal thoughts . . . the reborn woman of Tyre . . . the creator of angels and archangels . . . the mother of wisdom . . ."

The young man of the personnel group was very happy. The Brigadier had confirmed a suspicion. He had noticed the Brigadier's mental inflation, his obsession, the delusions of grandeur, that primordial power without end or beginning that is coupled with the woman who is both whore and wisdom. The Brigadier was in the grip of his archetype.

The Brigadier asked the young man's name and immediately ordered them to continue the tests. The young man answered the questions with ease, for he had suddenly gotten an insight into the matter — an insight into what was half abstract, and half concrete; half personal and half impersonal; into that which wavered between the actual and the symbolic.

*

Hope was busy serving tea to the hard-working young men of the D-Service. They had just completed the test by which they would be reclassified under the headings of action front and personnel group. As she went from one to the other, she good-naturedly put up with increasing assaults on her person.

The rose was pulled out of her hair, her blue garter was taken off and thrown about the room, her whole body became black and blue in the boisterous romp. But she was happy. She had divided the last of the powdered cantharides that she had gotten from her dear mother among the many cups. When the Brigadier, driven by unbearable lust and light-headed with delusions of grandeur, claimed the first right, she received from him as forfeit the exact address of Boris Gudenov — something that he had (perhaps on purpose) withheld from Captain Demosthenes de Goede.

Even the young men of the personnel group were excessive in their demands. She accepted the situation with understanding and compassion. There was life in the building — even if it could only last a short while. In the heat of the passion, knowledge attained carnal heights which even the centaurs could not emulate. The interlude between Eros and intellect was unparalleled   decadence was plainly a lack of passion; sterility found its counterpart in mind as well as body.

Tattered and torn, but blissfully happy, Hope reached her terrace house, surrounded by her children. She fed them with leftover food from the day before and then rested her weary body on the big double bed, while she made plans for the great task that lay ahead. She was still unsatisfied; the gnawing hunger could not be stilled; the creative urge was unappeasable and tortured her like Barbarella on the rack; she could have died of rapture, doomed, like all the dying, to die of what caused rapture.

*

The Brigadier lay alone in his apartment on his triple bed and mused about incidents that sometimes formed a pattern. His body was spent, but his spirit was alert.

Lou-Salome — a friend of Freud, the beloved of Nietzsche and Rilke — Jean Harlow and Bee-Bee-Doo had all died of uremic poisoning. They had wanted to be mistress, mother and madonna, and also slave, silence and the source. They all desired the seed, but there was no outcome. There was only the abortion that mocked the intention. They had developed by-products of urine in the blood, and that had led to cerebral edema, congestion of the brain. The symptoms were dullness of the eyes, headache and, finally, nausea.

*

Projected identification.

Boris told Iole about Bee-Bee-Doo while her dark eyes were fixed on him. He and Bee-Bee-Doo had often gone out together, years ago when she was at the height of her fame. She had been a remarkable person: she could assume a pose for a photograph in the middle of a conversation — her smile remained the same, the movement was carried out, her eyes were in stark communication with the invisible spectators in the lens aperture. Then she would resume the conversation and the warmth, temporarily switched off, was there again.

There was a sort of warmth that emanated from her, a body heat that blended with her perfume and even activated it. Some women had a chemical reaction that was not attractive, but in her case it was otherwise: she was a woman born to love and to excite a man's senses. An evening with her had been full of adventure and usually ended in the green rooms with green curtains surrounded by the ferns, flowers,

fish ponds and incense of an Arabian pleasure garden. But
she had been very fussy: there was never a crease anywhere,
or an instant of angry criticism. She appeared with every hair
in place and lay almost prudishly on the bed and waited . . .

Suddenly the perspiration began to pour off Boris Gudenov's
forehead. He could scarcely speak. He looked into Iole's eyes
and willed her to understand what he could not say. That was
not Bee-Bee-Doo! That was someone else lying there! It was
a Myrrha in myrtle green with eyes shining with love for
someone standing behind you. There was an old man waiting
behind you. Was it fetishism that made you want to destroy
her? It seemed as if she welcomed the blue bruises on her
body, the scandal of her flesh.

Iole took him in her arms. There were tears in her eyes, as
with a primitive, elemental intuition, she accepted and for-
gave the sufferings of the tycoon. He and she were one; and
she endured the impotent assault on herself in a moment of
mystic transcendency. She endured the pain and the vengeance until he became quiet, and calmed by her subconscious
perception, found the peaceful center of the whirlwind.

He told her of Bee-Bee-Doo's end while they were both
searching for their lost halves in each other's arms. They
found some comfort in the fact that, raised above the purely
erotic, heterosexual love was based on projection — the truth
of the apocryphal, that the woman became like the man, that
opposites were reconciled, that the unconscious was united
with the conscious. He told her about Bee-Bee-Doo's end,
and he seemed to take a vengeful delight in it. Life had begun
to tell on her; each morning it took longer to restore the rav-
ishment of the night before. He took a secret pleasure in seeing her less well groomed than before. After a long night, her

breathing was sometimes jerky, there was white in the corners of her eyes, fine red lines appeared everywhere as small veins burst almost imperceptibly. She often became refractory and forgot her words when the cameras began to roll. Her hair no longer had the required glint. Vague problems of life were ousted by little problems that went no farther than arms that were becoming too fat, wrinkles that could no longer be nourished away, eyes that would no longer shine without the aid of eyedrops.

All this time Iole held Boris Gudenov in her arms, and as she listened her heart was filled with sadness at the thought that, after fulfillment, the projected love of the troubadour died, and that after a while you did not need your lover anymore. Her heart wanted to break in the realization of the tragic truth that she had sensed: that the woman becomes aware of the man in her, and the man of the woman in him. While he was talking, the realization came hazily that he would become lost in wise reflections, and that she would drift farther away in the sharp light of reason which gave her, even at this moment, a premonition of the inevitable.

On her apple green bed, Bee-Bee-Doo did not look the same, Boris Gudenov told her. Even the bed looked different — perhaps more like those beds in cheap railway hotels, or like the green back seats of cars under the trees along the main road; or like the grass growing in the backyards of pubs. Former fans, seeing her close up, felt superior . . .

Then they found her in bed, naked and dead. Boris Gudenov wanted to describe her body, the exposed body of Bee-Bee-Doo without mystery, destroyed by the life she led, but Iole dissuaded him.

Boris was suddenly as young as she. Across the chastised

body she saw Boris in herself, she knew just how he must have felt years ago when he was young and could mock at women and their weaknesses — when he was strong — and she seemed to feel in herself that urge to live, and saw in herself the young man with the top buttons missing from his shirt, and felt the hot blood that drove him to exuberant living.

She laughed suddenly, and Boris Gudenov was blinded by her youth and beauty. She was the most beautiful girl he had ever seen. And then he laughed too, but he held his hand in front of his mouth as though he wanted to curb his laughter.

They ceased, as though they were newly aware of the tragedy — the tragedy of one who was moving away from the light, and the other who was moving toward it — the tragedy of a temporary meeting, where each borrowed from the other — the tragic interlude of an older man and a younger woman at the paradisal crossroads of similar sensitivity. And while they had laughed a moment before, they were now filled with sadness which at the same time brought them nearer together; and, in the presentiment of inevitable separation, made them realize, ironically enough, the strength of their growing union.

*

The rules of the game — and feminine mystique.

Katy's friends waited patiently for her to open her heart. They sprawled in expensive dresses on chairs designed by interior decorators, knees together and heels at an angle of forty-five degrees to protect the unmentionable garments against the assaults of fashion.

Unselfishly she told them about Boris and all the demands made on him. "And may I mention that my child and I also

suffer under all the obligations that his financial kingdom en-
tails, the work that he does for the public?"

For a woman to remain in the background was not the
modern idea. It was anathema, according to their debauched
views, and they shook their heads sadly in front of their hostess
who from time to time asked for advice without giving all the
direct details. They answered her equally indirectly in the
surreptitious game in which you revealed everything in a
roundabout way, and counted on getting solutions by cir-
cumlocution.

"All I want is love and humaneness," said Katy. "The pleasure of ordinary conversations, the joy of a companion who
could mend a broken chair, who even comes home drunk now
and then, who is home-loving, and for whom you would like
to do something. Someone who makes you feel important,
and who can appreciate you. Someone who likes people, and
whom people like. A normal man with a romantic imagination and a sense of humor. Is that asking too much?"

They took her hand and pressed it reassuringly.

"I'm not referring to Boris, of course," she added quickly.
"Boris is very good to us, even if we see him so seldom." They
assured her that they understood. No one would pass on a
word or an accusation as testimony, but they were all attuned
to the invisible image concealed behind their debauched view
of life.

"I'm longing," said Katy brushing her hair out of her eyes
and looking at her friends with large eyes like a young girl,
"for someone who likes to play with children, and who makes
you feel safe and reassured. But what can one do? A whole
world rests on his shoulders. We are very proud of him,
Hyllus and I."

They nodded in agreement. Katy's masochism was permissible according to the *regula ludi:* Boris was her lifespring, and even if he gave in to all the demands she made of him, she would not welcome the reconciliation. They could not imagine that she would find harmony tolerable; happiness was humdrum compared to the excitement of self-chastisement.

"I hate geniuses who snobbishly leave their stamp on society," said Katy hotly. "I hate men who in the race for power and wealth forget their obligations in the home."

Her friends agreed wholeheartedly. Each had her own troubles which vaguely resembled those of the others. They seemed to find a reassurance in the relationship. They prepared themselves to ply Katy with the sort of advice they would themselves like to receive on their own problems: not so much a solution to the problem, but an admission of injustice.

"Jack Gordon was asking after you the other day," said one, steering the game into its second phase — the problem of how much to allow the absent Jack without jeopardizing their own positions according to the rules.

"Sweet of Jack," said Katy moving her toes in her spike-heeled shoes in time to thoughts.

"Jack thinks you are irresistible," said another, and they drew their chairs closer together.

Jack had as many faces as there was need for: he was a mechanic, an Italian gigolo, a presumptuous teen-ager, or anyone that they desired illicitly.

"Jack says you are the prettiest woman he has ever seen," said another.

They smiled and brushed the hair out of their eyes, happy at the thought of the invisible someone for whom they wore the pretty panties, the lace underslips and the bras of finest transparent nylon, that suggested a focus of provocation, beautiful behind the mesh.

They all talked at the same time and chattered excitedly about the one who could not afford speedboats and Jaguars like their husbands, but knew how to use them. They warbled their longing for their composite, imaginary figure who achieved the impossible by combining youth with maturity, the one who tormented them with the ice-cold phallus of Azazel, the one before whom their soft, helpless, successful husbands became ridiculous eunuchs.

Katy was surrounded by her friends who comforted and supported her; fine women with the last vestiges of youth still in their poses and gestures, with the last traces of beauty that had to be carefully pampered; filled with a longing for the warm rain of love without the burden of fruitfulness. They were constantly in communication with the invisible incubus that had to satisfy them, and together with Katy, their hostess, they made such impossible imaginary demands that even the original Creator of ornament and cosmetics would have had to have recourse to artificial aid. The successful husbands could argue and reproach as they chose; they could not pacify the cold desire.

*

The old formula.

According to Andro Man of Aberdeen, 1597, you could conjure up your master, the devil, by calling *Benedicte!* The devil could be exorcised by catching the dog and putting him under your left armpit with your right hand, and filling his mouth with pebbles and saying, *Maikpeblis!*

THE LION

Something is here, something is next
to me, something is following me · The
dedicated ducktail and Minie went down the
escalator with Captain Demosthenes de Goede to
the floor below, where various departments branched
out in all directions from a central point. As he looked down
from the steps, even the Captain (a pilot in the Korean war)
felt dizzy, because there seemed to be no end to the man-
made abyss where invisible teen-agers banged drums and
twanged strings.

When they reached the bottom, they hesitated a moment,
which enabled a smart old gentleman in a snuff gray suit with
a gold watch slapping against his stomach to come up to them
from the corner where he had been keeping a secret eye on
them. He bowed to the Captain and asked in which direction
their interests lay. This was naturally a difficult question to
answer immediately, and the old gentleman laughed ho-ho!
behind his luxurious gray beard. He accompanied them,
his hand lightly on the Captain's arm, and he told them that
Gudenov policy was that the client should be left entirely free
to do what he liked. "We have the products," he said as he
cleaned his false teeth with his handkerchief, "and we are
proud of the fact that we can supply all needs." He put the
dentures back and laughed at the Captain, showing snow
white teeth. "The client is under no obligation, and if he
chooses he can spend his whole life wandering about here without buying anything."

Captain Demosthenes de Goede stopped next to one of the
bookstalls. He picked up a *Physique Pictorial* and began to
leaf through it casually. While he was looking at a nude cow-

boy with two revolvers on his bare hips, he nonchalantly asked the old boy, who was just as interested in the picture, "Do you happen to know Boris Gudenov?"

"Heard a lot about him," said the old fellow. He turned the pages of the book which was still in the Captain's hand, and showed him another picture of the muscular young man adjusting his belt.

Captain Demosthenes de Goede gave the dedicated ducktail and Minie a telling glance and, casually leafing on until he came to two wrestlers locked in an octopus hold, he asked, "Do you perhaps know where one can find Boris Gudenov?"

But the old man had taken down an *Amigo* and a *Strong Man* from the rack and was very busy showing the Captain other, more daring, photographs. Demosthenes de Goede repeated his question, and the old fellow took yet another magazine from the rack. "Look around and you will see his monument," said the old chap and laughed so boisterously that he had difficulty in keeping his dentures in place. He took the opportunity of polishing them again.

Captain Demosthenes de Goede looked with interest at a *Homophile Zeitschrift* that the old man had pushed into his hand, and fired a quick question, "When did you last see Boris Gudenov?"

"Never seen him," said the old fellow who had taken Demosthenes de Goede's arm. "Of course, Boris Gudenov is the name of a company, but I can't remember ever having seen a photo of the founder Boris Gudenov. There are enough photos of Bee-Bee-Doo, of course," he said bitterly, "but none of Boris Gudenov." He looked thoughtfully at the Captain who was skimming through the magazine and now looking at the illustrations with real interest. He suddenly darted forward and gave the Captain a smart pinch just above the pectoral muscle, looking inquisitively into his face for signs of pain. The only response he got was an expression of dumb amazement, and the old fellow was in ecstasy at these incredible signs of sadomasochism. He began to talk about leather, uniforms, shoes and discipline and found Captain Demosthenes de Goede really interested, until Minie succeeded in pulling him away and the dedicated ducktail, with a blow of his elbow, made the lewd old man curl up with lascivious pain.

"Narcissism is a pathological curse," said the dedicated ducktail steering the Captain toward the next hall, where six candidates of the shopworkers' union were bringing the nomination battle to a close by all appearing together beneath a fifteen-foot high picture of Bee-Bee-Doo on her deathbed. This was an annual occasion, and part of the Gudenov policy that client and employee must have a glimpse into each other's lives. Underneath the tortured face of the sex queen, all six speakers got a turn to speak for five minutes, and within that space of time to reconcile an image of selfless service with their own personal ambition.

They were rigged out in shop clothes: scrubbed and shaved automatons, built on the neomiddle-class pattern. They waved greetings right and left like boxers entering the ring and gave themselves up to the enthusiastic applause as though there was some special message in the cacophony; they responded to each display of enthusiasm as though the roar of the enormous crowd was a personal tribute to each one of them. They did not see the individual faces, but danced a ritual fire dance in front of the many-headed dragon, searching assiduously amongst the clichés of eloquence for the one magic word that would tame the monster. Six little men compelled to be opportunists; six puppets who would one day dominate the monster, the master. Each smile, each slavish concession, each small obligation in this puppet show was recorded on the debit side of the account that would one day be rendered. Six mannikins with a longing for greatness, warning against the Götterdämmerung that would follow if they were not accepted. Meanwhile they laughed and greeted their audience with a servility which they would one day avenge. Six mannikins, booted and spurred — ready to answer questions from the audience.

All selling was suspended until such time as the speeches should be finished; the plum was the question time, and after that the occasion would be celebrated with snappy service and exaggerated purchasing.

"Are you for or against the four-day week?"

"Are you for or against ecumenical philosophy in trade unionism?"

One of the speakers spied the robust figure of the Captain right in front, who slowly and clearly formulated his question: "What is your opinion with regard to Boris G. . . . ?"

The one who had to answer the question rose quickly, his face stern and earnest, his hand on his heart. "I am proud to say that I stand firmly behind our celebrated leader, Boris Goodman . . ." and his voice was lost in the shouts and cheers of the crowd who, jumping to their feet, totally drowned the repeated calls of the Captain, "GUDENOV! GUDENOV!"

After the enthusiasm and the tributes had calmed down and peace was restored, further questions were allowed. "What are your views on centralization?" — But the most important

question came from the little man in the white uniform, the
one charged with the image of the late lamented. He was
obviously the darling of the teen-agers. He was a real character and was still busy chewing his food. He washed it down
with a mouthful of tepid tea, and put his question, "What are
your feelings with regard to Bee-Bee-Doo?"

His voice was hardly audible in the renewed stamping of
the teen-agers who suddenly showed some interest.

"What do you feel about Bee-Bee-Doo?" the little man repeated his question and, depressed and hostile, listened for the
anticipated superficiality:

Bee-Bee-Doo was . . .

Bee-Bee-Doo was someone whose life testified to the abuse
of love; the tragic, treacherous nature of our life on earth.

The voice of the pop singer, Charles Aznavour, came over
the loudspeakers and repeated the theme. The teen-agers, in
blue jeans and parkas, in beatle boots and desert boots, in
duffel coats and baggy Levis, huddled around the invisible
central point of their gathering, gave an orgastic moan. Exhausted heads bowed, shoulders bent, they began imperceptibly to move, and changing from their characteristic pose of
controlled apathy, they broke into the quick rhythm of the
Frug, the canned formula of their protest. The dancing
ducktail, converted to the Christian neo-secular There-was-a-
God-but-God-is-dead, with Minie at his side, led Demosthenes de Goede away to the next hall, for the House of
Gudenov was large and there were many rooms.

*

Someone offered them wine; it was nomination day and
everyone was celebrating. The libations that were poured to

the accompaniment of bibulous laughter were zealously drunk by Captain D. de Goede, and he felt decidedly better. He could feel the liquor running through his veins, and he welcomed the cravings of the lion that now mastered him. He looked around for someone with whom he could come to blows (preferably the hound Gudenov), but all that he could see were the crowds milling between counters of perfume for men and women: glass cases full of preparations; Venetian bottles of colored extracts for armpits, pubic hair and per-spiration — anything to banish the odor of passion and energy. There was toothpaste, rinses for aging hair, pink prep-arations for dull gums, all the colors of Joseph's coat for eye shadow, spray for wet hair, scar removers, remedies against emotion, remedies for emotion, appetite stimulants, appetite killers, concoctions to conceal and dehumanize served by girls as pretty and as obliging as Brigadier Ornassis E.'s girls of the Service, and he could have roared with undefined rage and desire for action.

He glanced around the room and saw a fellow who looked like a cockatoo: a great fat windbag, dressed like a dandy, surrounded by an adoring crowd of girls who followed him backward and forward through the *parfumerie*. Captain de Goede went to meet him, his notebook ready, his sharpened pencil poised menacingly.

"Oo-la-la," said the scintillating dandy in an abnormally feminine voice that reduced his beauty chorus to giggles.

Captain Demosthenes de Goede put his question firmly in a clear voice, with the sensitive pride of one who had overcome a speech defect.

"Boris Gudenov," repeated the cockatoo, studying a cosmetic preparation, "is an enigma of our times. If there is any truth anywhere, then Boris Gudenov personifies the indecision of our findings. Double meanings and contradictions . . . is that what you want?"

Captain Demosthenes de Goede handled his pencil like a javelin, while the girls came closer, still giggling.

"Who is Boris Gudenov?" repeated the plumed fatso, uncorking the bottle. He smelled it and pulled his nose up. "Rabbi Uri said that he had four faces: one when he prayed, one when he learned, one when he ate, and one when he received visitors. In which face of Boris Gudenov are you interested, Mr. . . . ?"

"Captain Demosthenes de Goede," said the dedicated ducktail.

"Captain," said the fat gasbag inclining his head, but his eyes were fixed on the girls. Then he looked at the Captain standing there, awkward and out of place, with the pencil in his hand; but he also saw the powerful muscles, the splendid physique and the primitive simplicity which did not escape the notice of the girls. He put his hand to his side and felt the rolls that were hidden by his silk shirt.

"Or perhaps, Captain, you are interested in that aspect of Boris Gudenov that turns him into a romantic figure. The episodic brush marks on the canvas of his life, for which of us is really interested in problems?" His puffy hands stroked his hair, softly caressing the curls. "Boris Gudenov is a potentate of an extensive commercial network, a rajah of banking, a colossal corporate body in economic life." He came and stood close to the Captain, but he had to look up to him, and the rolls of his neck folded over each other. "He is a friend of princes; he has received *cadeaux d'estime* from kings and he is so powerful that he is even beyond the reach of his friends. But he has a weakness . . ."

The girls were giggling again.

The dandy pressed the Captain lightly on his arm.

"Boris Gudenov is the most hated man because he has all the power and luxury, and he is the closest to everyone because he is also the destruction of all illusions."

The dandy now teased the Captain with his pose of mock familiarity while he walked all around him as if he could not get enough of the vigorous figure.

"In a world that has become tired of the unattainable, it is fitting that someone like him should be an example of vulnerability among all the splendor and exotic trimmings of his status as a world tycoon."

The fat man looked at the Captain's uniform and made no attempt to control his laughter. He seemed to be performing a dance with his unwieldy body which nevertheless achieved spry and mincing movements; a colorful, foppish bird confronting an animal of the veld. He touched the leather jacket and tugged at the cheap shirt. Then he stood still, shaking his perfumed head.

"Can someone like you grasp that much?" he asked with affected melancholy in which the afterglow of sincerity shone for a second.

The Captain hit him, and received an unexpected karate blow in return that nearly lifted him off his feet. They were both immediately on their guard, instinctively as intellectual and athlete, conscious of the blunder of oversimplification. They hit, chopped and strained at each other without giving way an inch, while the girls were interested spectators. Every hold of the Captain's was answered by a counter-hold which was in a peculiar way, a perversion of the true hold; each enormous exhibition of strength on the part of the Captain was used against him by leverage action. When he was on the point of losing his self-respect forever, the Captain abandoned himself instinctively to the most primitive hold of all: a furious embrace in which, as though surrendering to love, you squeeze and squeeze your opponent as hard as you can. Perspiration ran off his forehead, he pulled his enemy against him until he hurt himself, and then the dandy gave in, while the girls crowded around and casually switched their alliance.

"A remarkable exhibition," said someone.

Demosthenes de Goede looked up and saw his friend of the Rolls-Royce, the one who looked vaguely familiar, with a beautiful girl on his left arm, dark, aloof and haughty. He still had his arm around the bruised ribs of his opponent who was panting for breath like an asthmatic. The dark girl came forward and softly loosened his hold. She wiped the sweat from the young man's face with a dainty handkerchief. The man also came between the two and said, "Rather let him be. It's not important." The fat dandy allowed a couple of girls to lead him to one of the counters like a conquered hero, where they laved and perfumed him with all the many preparations available. He leaned against the counter and his fat face suddenly creased into a smile under his alert eyes which twinkled in the Captain's direction. Then the smile broadened into an unbridled burst of laughter as he saw how his supporters clustered around the Captain's muscles. He sat down heavily on a chair and fanned himself with his sweet-smelling handkerchief, his fat body shaking with laughter that became more and more uncontrollable, in spite of his pain. Afterward he

was almost doubled up with laughter, and the tears were
streaming from his eyes.

"You are most welcome," said the man to Demosthenes de
Goede. "I hope you enjoy your visit." He nodded to Demosthenes de Goede while the dark girl joined him again. "If
we can help in any way . . ."

   Now the fat man was laughing so loudly that Demosthenes
de Goede could hear just about nothing. He tried to think,
he tried to rescue himself from this unaccustomed situation,
but his helplessness in the circumstances even made his
thoughts stupid. He looked at the man, the girl and the laughing windbag, and he tried with all the powers of his muscles
to think. He felt something pulsating against his temples. He
felt his limitations and traced them to something physical,
something that had, at times, prevented him as an athlete from
achieving those supernatural bursts of effort that time and
again gained him the laurel wreath at Olympiads. He followed
that impotence to the level of life as he knew it, as a policeman in his terrace house, with the enormous gulf between
authority and servant, caste against caste — all the ramparts
that separated one class from another, that meant more than
money, that was inconceivable and unintelligible. There was
nothing behind him but his strength; and in this case his
strength had proved nothing. There was another dimension
of thought here, a sphere where the heroic appearance and
gesture had no significance. Desperately he took refuge in his
work and the methods that would enable him to achieve his
task; he took out his notebook and held his pencil ready, a
puny thing in the great knout of his hand.

   "I would appreciate it," he said formally, mindful of the

Brigadier's approach, "if you could give me information about a person called Boris Gudenov."

"That's difficult," said the man. "Everyone has heard of Boris Gudenov, but what information exactly do you want?" He pressed the girl close to him. "Are you looking for Boris Gudenov as the dog, the nigredo who suggests misery, suffering and destruction, who lives in the deepest shadows of the soul's melancholy? Are you looking for the sickling and seeking his destruction, or are you looking for the Boris Gudenov who has shattered traditional images, who has given a new symbol to our times and by means of mass culture has shaped man according to mass average?" Captain Demosthenes de Goede considered the answer carefully. He looked around helplessly at the dedicated ducktail and Minie standing next to him, at the girls who were watching him in an admiring flock, and his thoughts seemed to bang up against that blankness that was the best disguise of all. Why was he here? What did he want here? He longed for the sort of world he had known, but which had changed before his very eyes.

The Captain seemed to realize for the first time that he was growing old, for there was something hovering on the threshold of realization to which he could give no words, and of which he had no clear, incisive idea. He suddenly felt alone, and became aware that he was cutting a ludicrous figure. He heard someone laughing. There was a clown in the shadows: it was here, it was there, it followed everywhere. He shook his head as if to shake himself out of a nightmare world. There was something in the confusion that could only be exorcised by tremendous self-discipline. To understand this present world of dreams and fantasy, there must be firm

ground under your feet; there must be understanding, otherwise for the rest of your life you would be doomed to empti-
ness and nothingness; otherwise you would become the victim
of the autonomous powers which could reduce you, by means
of their devilish arts, to their own nothingness. That was the
danger against which the Brigadier had warned him: something had to be brought to light; something had to take on a
tangible form so that it could be overcome by might and
reason.

Captain Demosthenes de Goede suddenly became calm. Although he knew nothing as yet, he was at least beginning to
get an idea of his task and all the dangers attached to it. He
listened with heartrending intensity to the amorphous conception churning at the back of his mind.

All at once the dedicated ducktail leaned nearer and whispered in the Captain's ear: "God is dead. We no longer rec-
ognize the Sacred, the Inviolable. There is nothing. There is
nothing but our earthly duties and Christian love for everyone and everything."

The Captain looked at the dedicated ducktail and then at
Minie. A light shone in her dark eyes which would help him
if he could understand it. There was something in her eyes
that he had seen in women just before he overwhelmed them
with sexual love, but he could not put his finger on it.

In the distance the trade union candidates had answered
their questions unsatisfactorily, and Bee-Bee-Doo's theme
song resounded through the building. The Captain listened
to the song, and it brought quite another conception, just as
formless. Something was at grips with something, and was
leading irrevocably to total destruction. There was a light in
Minie's eyes, and Captain Demosthenes de Goede was on the

point of getting an inspiration that would explain everything. But it just escaped him.

When he looked around again, the man with the familiar face had disappeared, and the whole situation had collapsed. The Captain was back where he had started. But still, there was something to hold on to: something is here, something is next to me, something is following me.

Captain Demosthenes de Goede followed his two companions through the halls of the shopping center, and he was followed in turn by the horde of girls. He was amazed at all the luxury; he was surrounded by people he met every day in the street: mothers with children, fathers and mothers, couples and groups; and then the lone wolf, the one with a beard or long hair, the affected walk of the deviate, the swaying gait of the alcoholic, the meanderings of the drug addict. The situation was normal, as he knew normality, but there was no sign of Boris Gudenov. At times the Captain thought he saw someone he knew: a face, the cut of a coat, a familiar movement; someone like one of his colleagues of the D-Service; faces that turned toward him, but then became unrecognizable because they were only familiar as types.

Here and there he stopped someone and asked about Boris Gudenov.

"Boris Gudenov is the power behind the scenes in every war," said a young man. "He sells arms to all, and he thrives on blood, but his day is over."

"Boris Gudenov is a Russian dictator who wants to rule the world," said another.

"Boris Gudenov is the socialistic ideal that will save the world."

The Captain stood next to a little girl sitting on the lap of the shopping center's Santa Claus and whispering her wishes into his ear while he ogled her mother and caressed her little thigh.

"Boris Gudenov is Father Christmas," said the little girl.

The Captain felt a yearning he could not understand. He was filled with longing for something that these people as devotees accepted mechanically; something that made him feel an outsider. He began to have doubts about himself: doubts about the heroic concept which had always been clear to him; he had to reconcile himself to an idea that was entirely opposed to his way of thinking: that true worthiness was no longer found in the proud sacrifice for a great cause, but in the meek acceptance of little things, for everything was small, there was no longer anything great. He suddenly stood, tired out, keeping his arm without thinking around Minie and his other hand on the dedicated ducktail's shoulder, while he tried with vacant eyes to see some significance in all the tumult.

They made a group on a platform before a portrait of Bee-Bee-Doo which took up a whole side of the wall, a tragic Venus elevated to form a canopy above the ladies' underwear department, on her face an expression of childish amazement, caused by inexpressible suffering, trapped by the camera for all time; an example of womanly allure according to the rules of the game into which she had been forced; swathed in green gauze which accentuated her curves, 35-24-35, with insertions of black velvet to mask three secrets in three places.

*

Captain Demosthenes de Goede walked slowly through the halls, followed by the girls and accompanied by the two teen-

agers. Buying was again in full spate, although the nomina-
tions struggle continued in canvassing on the floor, where
employees and customers both took part. There was a festive
air about the place, but the possibility of violence lay just below the surface. The slightest inflection of the voice or the
equivocal word could start an argument or unleash trouble.
It was like a boiling river, deep on the one side where the water
bubbled up from the unknown depths of the human psyche,
and shallow on the other where it formed tepid waves of over-
sensitivity and easy offense.

"It's the heat," someone said.

"It's the drought and the result of the credit squeeze," said
another.

The clerks' collars oppressed them; their shirts were rum-
pled with sweat.

The Captain saw a man who had too little money to buy
the things he wanted. The Captain followed him from hall
to hall as he went from one department to the other, his
mouth watering when he saw something tempting: a beach
jacket, a tie, some special expression of his vanity that was always just beyond his means. He was ready to commit murder
from frustration at the destruction of his daydreams, the
vision he had conjured up of himself on a crowded beach with
that tie around his neck, that Onyx perfume in his vicinity,
those cuff links in his white shirt — the vision in which he
was raised above the banality of his everyday existence. He
was a potential thief, but the Captain was hindered by his
instructions from coming into the open and acting to protect
the community.

Captain Demosthenes de Goede, the dedicated ducktail,
Minie and the girls went from hall to hall on a search that

every moment became emptier. It was like walking in circles on the hot sand of a desert surrounded by mirages, which they immediately recognized as mirages.

The dedicated ducktail suddenly had an inspiration.

"Who are you looking for?" he asked Demosthenes de Goede.

"I am looking for the hound," said the Captain, and the clown laughed in the distance.

At once the song of Bee-Bee-Doo became louder, for they had reached the next hall, and everyone was listening to the little man in the white jacket who was continuing his endless lectures.

"She was very beautiful, but she had her troubles," he said.

"She was very sensitive, and could feel at once if the people in the room were well disposed toward her."

He swallowed his lukewarm tea and looked calculatingly at his audience.

"They made her a symbol of feminine attraction; she allowed herself to be molded like clay, she lay bare for the sake of the image of the tragic Venus, but she was unhappy."

His thoughts became weak, like his tea, but he was encouraged by the message that was repeated over and over again. "She often doubted her own talents because she realized that the role had been created for her. She never wore underclothes. Her clothes were transparent. One night at a party she danced on the drums in her green frock — and then stripped."

The little man swallowed his tepid tea, cleared his throat and spat into his handkerchief.

"She followed her men like a lamb, and endured their assaults."

He completed the first half of his speech which would be continued in the next hall. Meanwhile he sold photographs of Bee-Bee-Doo which were not in the least pornographic. One could see nothing improper: just her face, portions of her breasts, thighs and a smile aimed impersonally at everyone. Shiny photographs of the feminine figure as something to be scorned; glossy prints that were boring rather than a temptation.

Bee-Bee-Doo's song resounded through the hall as Demosthenes de Goede tried to find Boris Gudenov. He went from hall to hall while the subtleties of her voice escaped him. He was a large man, blessed with strength and firmness of purpose, and as a police champion for the community, he was adjusted to obvious decadence: the Sahara of the soul, blasphemy, the crime against the order. But his impotence and anger increased because he could find nothing but tedium, boredom, barrenness and sometimes a specific crime that violated a principle but against which he could do nothing, on instructions from Brigadier Ornassis E. He was filled with anger, like a lion that could not see his enemy. And, because he was a man of action, his anger grew with each frustration and piled up against the mysterious Boris Gudenov who was the personification of it all.

Captain Demosthenes de Goede was ready for action against the enemy. The enemy was here, there, everywhere. His wrath was switched on, his muscles bulged, he arrested the man who had stolen a bottle of *Signature* men's cologne — but let him go at once when he remembered his instructions. He shouted his fury and frustration to the gilded dome of the shopping center and moved farther down, floor after floor, to the bottom, to the source of sound and trouble, of everything that he did not understand — because something is here, something is next to me, something is following me.

*

Report.

Brigadier Ornassis E. had had an outstandingly good night's rest, and looked at his brilliant young men from both departments with clear eyes, which immediately put them all on their guard.

"Has anyone seen Mrs. de Goede?" he asked.

No one could give any information, and the Brigadier tapped on his desk with his pencil. He ordered one of the young men to turn the record player down a trifle.

"Who are they?" he asked.

"David and Marianne Damour," said a young man of the personnel group.

"I don't like it," said the Brigadier. "Too little social comment."

The record was changed for one of Nick Taylor's.

A couple of girls from the Service went and sat on the floor on either side of the Brigadier and leaned their heads against his knees. The Brigadier rubbed their heads absentmindedly, and assumed an expectant attitude.

One of the men rose.

"Two members of the action front and one from the personnel group followed the Captain. He was involved in a fight which he brought to a successful conclusion. He held a short conversation with Boris Gudenov. He was beginning to take an interest in Bee-Bee-Doo, but was showing signs of increasing tension."

The Brigadier lifted his face to the light.

Another young man stood up (the one from the personnel group who showed exceptional promise).

"We think Captain de Goede has moved beyond the sphere of conscious emotional perception and is experiencing the first indications of primordial awareness."

"Of course," said the Brigadier impatiently, trying to free his hand which had become entangled in the intricacies of a beehive hairdo. Tears of pain welled up in the girl's eyes, but she smiled bravely, as behooved a member of the Service, when the Brigadier freed his hand with an impatient tug and held out his glass for a few drops of Rémy-Martin Cognac.

"The question is, naturally," said the young man with exceptional ambition, "whether the Captain, as an ordinary soul, is capable of taking in the significance of his archetypes."

The Brigadier gave a cruel snigger which doomed the ambitious young man, to the great delight of the others, to the action front for the rest of his career. He had a good deal of trouble in freeing his left hand in spite of a couple of impatient tugs which he made as unostentatiously as possible. He frowned as a faint scream came to his ears, and the girls of the D-Service exchanged significant glances. The sunny beach at Clifton would be waiting for Maureen Jones.

"Are you perhaps under the impression that it was our intention that someone like the Captain should interpret his own visions?" asked the Brigadier impatiently, his left hand motionless and hopelessly entangled in the loveliest golden hair in the Service.

The young man sat down, dismayed, and the Brigadier allowed a few more drops of Rémy Martin in the glass held in his free hand.

"What worries me most," said the Brigadier while the tension grew and the young men of the Service with the greatest effort kept their eyes turned away from his left hand, "is that Boris Gudenov is slipping farther and farther out of our reach. He allowed a brilliant young man to fill up his glass; and then the Brigadier did something that demonstrated his greatness and raised him above all other brigadiers of the lesser services. He jerked the shining hair on Maureen's tortured head so that she screamed like a kitten, and he looked straight at the brilliant young men who, smartly erect, were waiting for him to speak.

"Someone," said the Brigadier, "is unraveling Boris Gudenov's images and enabling him to find his own identity in the confusion."

"It's that girl Iole," said a young man of the action front who rose slowly, walked up to the Brigadier and with a lightning movement let a golden lock fall beneath his penknife's slash while he filled his chief's glass to overflowing.

"Exactly," said the Brigadier and looked with astonishment at the young man who, in spite of all the tests, had been so strangely misplaced. "One can only hope that, like most women, she will refuse to return the projected past."

The Brigadier put his shapely palms together and brooded absentmindedly. It was a sign to the young men that the greatest danger was past, and they filled their own glasses and began to talk to one another.

After three more glasses the Brigadier again asked if anyone had seen Hope de Goede. All affirmed their ignorance, and the Brigadier shrugged his shoulders.

"The shopping center need not necessarily be a fatal example in the ordinary sense," he said after a while. "It is we who see devilish apparitions in things because we can't reconcile ourselves to the side of our psyche that we constantly fear." He appealed to his young men. "And Captain de Goede is supposed to be without fear, isn't he? Was I not justified in my choice?"

They all hastened to reassure him.

"Boris Gudenov shall not win!" bellowed the Brigadier suddenly.

Again he was in a particularly difficult mood, and the young men felt their way uncertainly, trying to restore the peace.

"We dare not risk any form of desecration," said the Brigadier.

The clever young man from the action front came forward.

"There is always Bee-Bee-Doo," he comforted his chief.

The Brigadier shook his head. His better judgment confirmed the surmise: everyone was open to the secular ideas of the hound, Gudenov.

He listened to the record player.

"Johnny Congos and Keith Blundell," explained a young man of the personnel group.

The Brigadier hummed a folk tune and drank his cognac. "Have you ever wondered who Bee-Bee-Doo really was?"

"The one who through the ages moved from one body to another by metempsychosis and called all to the sowing of the seed," repeated a young man of the personnel group.

The Brigadier waved an impatient hand. "I mean, who was she with regard to Boris Gudenov?"

A young man looked at his notes. "His paramour . . . ?" he ventured.

Brigadier Ornassis E. held his head in his hands and waged a silent battle until he had regained his calm.

"May the All-Wise preserve us," he muttered, and took a sip of Rémy-Martin. He looked at Maureen Jones who sat next to him with bowed head, an expelled nun in secular clothes, with a small patch of white skin revealed on the top of her head; the thought of Clifton, muscular young men, photographs in the Sunday papers, dances, writers and their bacchanalia, sports cars, yachting adventures, the lotus existence beneath the slopes of the mountain, the bitter enjoyment of a beautiful body and the malaise of youth, a shocking contrast to the deeper and worthier demands of the Service. She wept silently for the Paradise lost forever: the desire of all beautiful girls to give themselves up, unnoticed and in silence, to exalted and worthy ideals.

The Brigadier wanted to stroke her head, but had second thoughts. Better, perhaps, that she should wage her battle alone, in silence, and doing penance.

"No," said the Brigadier to the young man. "With regard to the part that they have to play toward one another: the Prounikos and the sick king; the slut and the impotent man. It has come to my notice that there are certain fools in our Service who do not grasp the significance of Bee-Bee-Doo in the shopping center . . ."

Even the young men from the action front seemed surprised.

"There are even some who expect Captain Demosthenes de Goede to give us in his search a detailed portrait of the tycoon . . ."

A few members of the personnel group began to laugh, cautiously at first, then more loudly as soon as they saw that the Brigadier was smiling himself.

"And," said the Brigadier, "that some, perhaps from the action front, quite possibly even a couple from the personnel group, expect form and cohesion . . ."

The Brigadier was all smiles, and the young men realized that the danger was past.

"There is nothing logical," said the Brigadier ponderously, "and there is nothing that is unlogically logical. In the Gudenov world everything is uncohesive and amorphous. It is the snare of someone like Boris Gudenov, and it is our duty, as members of the Service, to search and to see if there are not perhaps traces, in the secular chaos, of a metaphysical significance, or whatever it is."

The Brigadier drained his glass of Rémy-Martin, and did not protest when someone offered to refill it.

"Our danger," said the Brigadier, "lies in the fact that Boris Gudenov, the creator of everything secular, will detect a pattern, something that will raise his existential chaos to a form, a materialistic myth, which will lure us, with our involuntary urge for uniformity, to compliancy."

He looked approvingly at his young men who were diligently taking notes. Then he allowed them to ask questions. There was only one question, and that came from one of his ablest young men in the personnel group.

"Where does Boris Gudenov sleep?"

The Brigadier looked from one young man to the other; it was clear that they had been halted before those annoying problems that often look unimportant, but are indeed important because members of the Service are expected to know everything.

Another young man came forward respectfully.

"A newsletter from the Academy. We hear that you have been proposed as the secretary of the ad hoc commission to study degeneration." The young man handed the newsletter to the Brigadier. "May I, on behalf of the members of the Service, offer you our hearty congratulations?"

There was loud applause from the rest of the personnel.

The Brigadier acknowledged the applause with a slight nod and looked at his portrait with the caption: "Snappy dolls in the Academy will have to look sharp to keep ahead when Brigadier Ornassis E. (photo above) tackles his new job with the devil's own energy."

The Brigadier was still a faculty member; he hoped later to become a full member. He also cherished the anticipation of an Academy award on the grounds of his work in the sphere of degeneration.

The meeting ended and everyone sang folk tunes until the Brigadier became sleepy and made signs to one of the young men to lead him to his room.

On the way to the door he said, "One must guard against rowdiness."

The young men grasped at once that it was an anti-corrective for the corrective laxity that they were sometimes allowed, to alleviate the discipline of their thought and way of life.

At the bedroom door the Brigadier asked, "Where is Hope?"

He stopped the young man who was going to reassure him.

"I think Hope is dead," said the Brigadier. "I've got a hunch. It follows me everywhere. It's a p-r-e-m-o-n-i-t-i-o-n."

The young man poured him a nightcap of Rémy-Martin Cognac. The Brigadier was reluctant to sleep. He wandered around the room and made a confidant of the young man (the clever one from the action front).

"They once asked Borges what death was," said the Brigadier, "and Borges said: 'Death is a city.'"

He looked at the young man in vain. He had not really earned promotion and did not understand a thing. But the Brigadier saw that the young man was well built — a young Apollo.

"Hope is dead," said the Brigadier, and motioned to the young man not to leave.

*

The zonah.

Hope, surrounded by her four children, was on her way to Gudenov's palace. In her mind's eye she saw Oita with its golden domes among the daffodils; she saw herself as the chosen vessel that would relieve the Archon from the light; she had come from the higher cosmos into this banal world, the spirit of woman, from far and wide. She had dressed herself as she imagined the pneumatological beings of the air: in shining white; her four children, descendants of Cain, promoted in pale blue to the lineage of Seth. They fought furiously against the frills and furbelows in which their mother had confined them; they were repeatedly impelled with claps in the bizarre procession through the city's tarred streets in broad daylight. It was an extraordinary procession that drew the attention of everyone as it passed the terrace houses, while the neighbors peered through the windows or leaned over their garden gates. She moved on with dignity, her long dress dragging on the asphalt, her hair streaming in the wind and her bright blue eyes seeing only visions of salvation.

In her hand she held a vial of gold with a stopper of lapis lazuli to suit the occasion. The precious liquid was the last Hope would ever receive from her beloved mother, for she

had recently died behind the glass walls of Welgevonden, comforted in her last hours by the background music for *"From
Crystal with Love."* It was the strongest excitant of all, orig-
inating from faraway Mexico: DAMIAN.

It was a long journey, but she managed it with greater ease
than her husband, Captain Demosthenes de Goede. She found
the correct entrance immediately, moved through passages
filled with antique furniture and opened one door after another
without knocking. She saw a group of women drinking tea
together who gave piercing shrieks as they perceived her over
their teacups; she saw a large dining hall with silver candelabra,
a reception room, and bedroom with silken hangings; she
moved from room to room among the costly pieces collected
from all parts of the world until she reached the last door. She
opened it and saw the handsome man with a girl in his arms,
his eyes blind with fear.

*

Beloved enemy.

Boris Gudenov and Iole walked through the large room with
an unhampered view over the city. After the hubbub of the
shopping center, from which they had just returned, it was
quiet and secluded here in his bedroom. He told her about
Bee-Bee-Doo's last years, and how they went together one
day for a swim in a lake next to a wood. Waterweeds
clutched at her legs, but it was really her desire for death that
he had to fight. Later when they lay exhausted beneath a tree,
he tried to talk to her and to understand something about it.
But they might just as well have been on different banks.
Nothing made sense to him; everything that had been compli-

cated at first had now disappeared in the simple fact of disintegration, which had been carried so far that the original causes
could no longer be discerned, nor were they of any further
importance. There was probably nothing that made one feel
more alone and helpless than when someone was reconciled to
his own destruction and waited with apathy for the end.

"And yet she wanted to take me with her," he told Iole.
"All her life she jeered at me, but at that moment she wanted
to wipe me out as well as herself."

Boris Gudenov stood with his back to the window, right in
front of Iole of the dark eyes.

"But what did she want to tell me? What did she want from
me, and what was it she wanted to do for me?"

He was a handsome man, very attractive to women until
they learned to know him. He was years and aeons older than
Iole who at this fleeting moment was nearer to him than any
woman had ever been.

"But I unmasked her at the last moment," said Boris Gudenov. "She was a character out of the *Ladies' Home Journal*.
She was as empty as those cookies and tarts in the shiny advertisements. She was completely under my spell. Bee-Bee-
Doo was nothing. I took over her image and made use of it.
Bee-Bee-Doo was the creation of Boris Gudenov, and nothing
more. She was the sick image of teen-age desire, she was the
girl who died on the pillion of a motorcycle, she was the
shadow who echoes their songs. When she died, I let myself
be photographed with her like all the others."

It was difficult to say how much Iole understood when she
took Boris Gudenov in her arms. In spite of the relatively
short duration of their relationship, which they both now

looked upon as temporary, they were in other respects perfectly adjusted. Iole had a mystic message, born of love, which she would reshape within a few years into definite opinions; Boris Gudenov was filled with sadness when he realized that he had made use of her in the same way that he had all his life made use of everyone and everything.

But now there was something — something that was following him, that was always with him, that would allow him no rest. Boris Gudenov as tycoon was — perhaps more than anyone else — conscious of order and design based on economic, biological and psychic laws. His pragmatic judgment had never failed him in the past. But he suddenly had a desire, such as never before, for something from the time of his grandfather, the *Maggid*, hidden in the mists of his youth.

He looked over Iole's shoulder while her warm breasts pressed against him. The abstract design on the curtains was part of the décor. Then, suddenly, patterns began to form in the design: a mocking face, Pan with an indescribably evil countenance. He could feel himself being overcome by fear, and enduring the fear as long as he could, he seemed to welcome the moment of madness, until the discipline of his will forced the plurality of forms and shadows back into the abstracts which served as decoration alone.

Iole's head rested on Boris Gudenov's shoulder. There was a look of inexpressible happiness on her face.

Boris Gudenov pulled himself together. His empire and all that it had brought with it had raised him above the cares of ordinary people. He was not as lonely as other tycoons, nor did he have a phobia for invisibility, such as Kirsch, Huntington and others who had tried to buy immortality. He took a pride in all the work he had achieved; the dark, unfamiliar part of his psyche was a world that had to be overcome. Even the fear of a moment ago was something that he could control; the desire that rose in him was only a passing fancy for those things of his youth that were now strange to him; whatever it was that was following him, that would not leave him in peace, was something he had to bring to light, something to which he must give a name.

Iole stroked his hair and rubbed her cheek against his.

Boris Gudenov was a name with magic powers. He could make those mysterious things come to heel; the searchlight of his reason could blind those psychic monsters.

While he was drawing Iole closer to him and caressing her, lost in thought, he saw his room in front of him with a sudden clarity: the arrivé effects he had suffered architects to contrive under the impression that they had a true conception of luxury. He looked at the walls hung with costly tapestries, the many adornments: the altarpieces, the credenzas, the suits of armor, the ikons. He looked down at Iole and saw the sweet retarded smile of love. As he looked up, he perceived how the door slowly opened and a woman's figure appeared between the altarpieces, surrounded by four children, a *q'desjáh* in white, a vision from the days of the kings, with grotesque makeup that was like blasphemy in contrast to the innocence of the woman in his arms. It was a cabalistic vision standing in front of him: it was Ashtoreth with the vial of love in her hand. Petrified, he looked at her, and he seemed to relive the fear-patterns of his youth, for he saw, in the shadows behind, the image of Azazel and, farther back, the demon woman Lilith.

The mighty Gudenov strained his powers of reason to the utmost to exorcise the apparition. He looked around: there hung the constellation of Shemhazai, upside down, in the bright light. He concentrated with all the remarkable power available to him, then looked before him again, freed by his willpower from the chimera, and saw the zonah, painted like a whore and surrounded by her urchins. He was free from the specters of his imagination, but now up against a reality more grotesque.

Hope approached uncertainly, while her four children, overwhelmed by the luxury around them, clutched at her dress in terror. The world she had created for herself collapsed, the terrace house was back: forgotten now was the Brigadier and the lofty influence of his organization; without her husband Hope was now a woman alone, with a purpose that she no longer understood properly and which had suddenly become banal and meaningless. The light in the room seemed to worry her; she passed her hand over her forehead and looked around helplessly. What had she wanted to say? Why was she here? The old masters on the walls glinted and overwhelmed her; the period furniture offered no refuge; she did not know what to do, where to stand or where to sit — when to sit, or what to do with her children. The four, who in other circumstances would have immediately begun their demolition tactics, coped more easily with the strange situation. They looked hesitantly around, jostled each other and released her. Four little figures in cheap blue moved in four different directions. They tested the small tables, the chairs and touched the ornaments; they pulled their dirty little fingernails through the paint of Raphael, Titian and Botticelli; a Houdon bust shattered into fragments on the floor.

Hope stood under a chandelier. She tried to stop her children and stumbled over a 1777 fire iron, designed by the Comte d'Artois; her soft behind landed against a Marie Antoinette marble fireplace, smuggled out of the Bagatelle; the Viking hair refused to remain styled and cascaded over her eyes and shoulders. Pathetically she brought out her last weapon against this man whom she had recognized, but who now suddenly looked strange and different. She swayed her hips provocatively as she approached in her long dragging dress. Halfway, she realized that in this setting, in front of that lovely girl with her proud air, she looked a fool. With each step she felt more ridiculous without knowing exactly what was wrong. She hesitated, but went bravely on, trying in vain to weep. It would have been easier if she could have raised some tears, but something far back in the past had deprived her of the ability to weep. She was now in front of the unreachable couple and was conscious of the crushing contrast between her shiny dress and the expensive, simple material that suited Iole's self-assurance so perfectly. While her children messed up a Giorgione, she proffered the vial, handing over, as a gift, her only weapon.

Boris Gudenov received it with elegance, and in his eyes (free now from the fear with which he tormented himself) there was a trace of understanding and sadness. But only for a moment, because immediately the tycoon's ability to handle an awkward situation asserted itself.

He took her by the arm, led her to a chair covered in Beauvais tapestry and allowed her to sit down clumsily. A hidden bell had already summoned his valet who now received low-voiced instructions. He rounded the children up deftly and led them away to the adjoining room. Boris Gudenov, still holding the vial, bridged the momentary gap of embarrassment with small talk until his chauffeur appeared with the children who already had hold of his cap and were skipping elatedly around him. Boris Gudenov first asked Hope for her address, but then anticipated her answer by suddenly remembering the street and the number of their terrace house. At the door he gave the chauffeur instructions to take the whole family — good friends of his — for a little drive first, in the direction of Chapman's Peak, maybe — wherever they wanted to go. When they had all been led away and the door had closed behind them, he returned to Iole and suddenly realized that the vial was still in his hand.

He drew the stopper out and smelled it. Then he looked at Iole who was worshiping him with her dark eyes. He saw her lithe and beautiful, full of promise for all the years that lay ahead; her body supple and young, ready to surrender to the onslaughts of love. He smelled the vial again and walked over to the liquor cabinet where he poured out a glass of wine for each of them. As he was bending forward, he saw himself in the mirror, and examined his reflection thoughtfully. He went over each little wrinkle, each line of destiny that had developed with his financial empire, each scar of the Fates through the years. Over his shoulder he could see Iole in the glass, and he again saw the vision of the old man and the young woman — Salome in Elia's shadow. He made a quick decision and divided the contents of the vial between the two glasses.

At first, he experienced a feeling of sadness as he went toward Iole, his beloved. As a tycoon he had often been obliged to make difficult decisions. He was used to weighing up the facts against one another and often tipped the scale with a shred of presentiment that was not based on reason. For that moment he had always been in the hands of something autonomous, something that he allowed to take possession of him, something from the depths of his psyche. From that possession, from that surrender, he often received the answer. But it was a risk that someone like him had to take all his life. Only afterward, when everything had become clear, did others follow him.

He went to Iole and, looking into her eyes, offered her the glass. All that he saw was love, surrender and trust. She had made herself utterly submissive as the vessel for the sacred transformation. While they drank, he kept his eyes fixed on her, and then took her in his arms. As she pressed softly against him, he thought of all the possibilities that he had willingly and wittingly set in motion: the inhuman urges, the animal sex rages, the unbridled passions. It was a calculated risk, true to the nature of someone like Boris Gudenov who had built his empire with human souls as well as tangible material. But there was also the promise; fruition, reshaping, redemption.

It was perhaps the biggest risk he had taken in his whole career, for he had also staked his weakness, the sickness in himself that had become a symbol of decline. It was the fate of one such as he that the demands made on him became greater and greater, that the true disclosure was only granted to the one who took that risk.

He pressed Iole closer to him, as though he wanted to protect her as well as himself against the inevitable. Then the perspiration began to bead on his forehead as, surrounded by his *objets d'art*, enveloped in his creation the shopping center, he became caught up in the struggle from which he would not emerge unscathed.

*

Iole lay alone in the room. She lay on a Bukhara rug under a Velasquez. The marble eyes of Pan, sculpted by Francesco Laurana, were blind to her suffering. Her young body, tensed like a bow, weltered blood — stained in the grip of the lion that had overcome her and her invisible lover. Invisible — for the room was empty. There was no sign of the older man of wisdom. She was surrounded by Fra Angelico, Fra Filippo Lippi and Piero della Francesca — an Annunciation, a Madonna and Child, and a Crucifixion — the relics of a bygone Renaissance.

*

The gift.

Katy, surrounded by her friends, told them the story of Neuman Nessos and his death at the hand of Boris Gudenov. She sent Hyllus to fetch the gown, and she exhibited it. She held it against the light to show the bloodstains that like memories had become more firmly fixed with the years and had taken on fresh nuances. It was the will of Providence, it was tyche, stronger than all of us, it was the inevitable that destroyed everything and changed our whole future. She told it movingly and wept with her friends who were also victims in their own lives of the unfathomable.

They wept over the gown, touching the material and their own memories. Tragedy lay hidden in something like a gown, a handkerchief, or an almost perished garment. Somewhere in a drawer or a wardrobe there lay, or was hanging, a memento of a moment that the wailing women recalled with misty eyes. They romanticized while they felt the gown with long fingers; and they wept a little as they compared the inurement of their advancing years with the unrecognizable wonderful soft world in the distant past, protected by the hymen.

They hastened to give their hostess advice. She must be protected: against the weakness of a man who was aging and losing his contact with reality; against the impersonal world of contemplation; against someone who had forgotten what the true desires of a woman were. They burdened her with suggestions, until Katy herself, with sudden insight, thought of the significant gesture. She would send the gown to Boris Gudenov. It would be a gesture of forgiveness; it would be his last chance to rehabilitate himself for his own sake.

The idea was greeted with great enthusiasm. But the gown must be sent without stains; it must be a new beginning, an opportunity for transformation, a new garment for metamorphosis, a significant transfiguration where everything out of the past must contribute to the transformation. A serving maid was summoned, sent away, and she returned with a highly volatile but extremely effective stain remover. The women all gathered around Katy and helped her with the symbolic task until the mantle shone like new, and the stains had vanished forever in the evaporation of the fumes. Then Hyllus was called to hand it over to his father with a message from his mother. No! Without the message, because if Boris Gudenov could not himself understand, if he could not himself see the significance, the message would be meaningless.

They gave young Hyllus charge of the mantle and sent him to search for his father in one of the rooms of Oita, where he was most probably busy working with his typist.

"But remember to knock first," said Katy while her friends gasped.

For the first time the chorus was silent before the courage

of their hostess. And then, after the silence, their voices soft
and appreciative laved her with their profound homage.

*

Presentation.

Young Hyllus had no need to look for his father, because he
knew exactly where the strange, fascinating game had taken
place. He opened the door without knocking, and looked at
the girl lying on the Eastern rug in a small bundle under a large
painting, as though utterly spent. He approached cautiously,
and then seemed to sense the presence of other children in the
room. He looked around but saw nothing. He looked again
at the soft woman at his feet. He bent down and touched
her. Her skin was damp, her eyes closed.

He put the mantle to one side on the floor, and went and
lay next to her. He curled up against her, his young body
against hers, and he felt how her arms folded around him while
her eyes were still shut. He stayed like that, as he had seen his
father, the old man, do, and fell asleep.

When he awoke, he picked up the parcel and sauntered out
of the room, down the passage until he reached the sanctum of
his father, Boris Gudenov — the glass room that now looked
totally different. He found his father illuminated by seven
candles burning on his desk and surrounded by all his books.
He handed over the mantle and stood back a little to observe
the reactions and to get further information to carry to his
mother.

Boris Gudenov looked at his son with unseeing eyes. He
held the gown in his hand and looked at it equally blindly.
Then he smiled suddenly and gave Hyllus a fleeting kiss on his

forehead. A moment later he thought about it, and put the mantle on. He waited until Hyllus had left the room and shut the glass door, which locked automatically, behind him. He sat down again.

He gave a final wave to his son — such a typical product of his mother. He leaned with his elbow on the desk and inspected his young offspring, then promptly forgot him as he moved his arm three inches from the open flame.

He thought of all the years past, and saw himself as a young boy in the marketplace of that distant village he had never seen since, and which through the years had grown in his imagination into a place that did not exist. At which stage did the market, the peddlers, the old men with their long beards and the candlelit evenings disappear? He remembered, too, that early time when he was young and strong, and slept in the haystacks with the gay young girls. They could count as many stars as they liked, for the urge of the young lion in him was endless. What was it that filled one with higher ambition? At exactly what stage did he perceive his strange capabilities? Why had he sacrificed everything for all those tasks that had elevated him above other people?

He looked at the seven candles burning softly, and smelled the volatile vapors rising from the ridiculous cloak. It no longer mattered to him if, to some people, he was the hound, the symbol of evil; or if he was the genius who represented the spirit of the age, and who satisfied all their needs by means of his shopping center. He felt a nostalgia for the past, yet did not want it back. He felt sick and tired and finished. He was Doris Gudenov, and he was the shell that had to produce the pearl.

Life thrummed through him. Each minute he felt more strongly the demoniacal powers that could waft him away in their flight, although he knew that ecstasy was of as short a duration as intoxication and moments of inspiration. The little human desire that was left could no longer be accepted as such, because it had to become part of the great current; it had to be woven into something that fitted into the inescapable pattern, the sound of the piccolo in the great orchestra.

The candles flared as they had done in the room of his childhood: with crooked and unpredictable flames.

Perhaps your whole life is one great participation. Just like Bee-Bee-Doo who also slept with young men in haystacks — a small-town slut plucked by the greater powers out of her little place and shaped, like you yourself, to fit into the still fluid pattern that was being formed out of the dark, unrecognizable past.

He longed to have the simplicity of his enemy, Demosthenes de Goede, who would eventually also go to his ruin against the higher powers; he hated his own perceptiveness that made everything insipid and robbed him of his conceit and pride.

He longed for a state of madness when he would be helpless in the grip of primitive forces; he preferred even the fear of darkness; he wished that he could become the victim of that ominous something that was following him, that was always next to him.

He thought of Iole, and his thoughts shuttled back and forth, and nothing seemed to make sense any longer. In spite of what had happened, Iole was all at once the unfathomable silence, the globe, the mist, the still white moon, the golden eyes, the sweet fragrance of holiness, the fire and the passion, something that flamed, and everything in contrast and she came like the moon across the plains and over the mountains and trees, and through the silver light between the eastern hills . . .

She came, Iole, for a moment only, at the crossroads. And it did not matter any longer whether he had lost or won. He thought with longing of all those things that formed a hopeless part of his desires and suddenly saw the sleeve of his cloak catch fire, set alight by the seven white candles of his almost forgotten past.

THE BLACK WOLF

Lupus Niger — putrifactio, mortifi-
catio, separatio & furens • Captain Demosthenes de Goede heard the bells of the
orchestra as the Kallman Choir was singing "Peter
Gunn." A blonde, a brunette, a redhead and a woman
with chestnut hair found words to fit the strange music that
accompanied the procession. They came through the hall,
the bearers, who with a swaying movement, continually
changed the picture before the eyes filled with the fear of
death. There was a scent of *Onyx* around the bier; there was
a silk tie hiding the face. No one moved in the hall; the
counters formed one solid image after the other before the
frightened eyes. Above them was the golden dome, flaming
like the sun; with each swaying movement the rococo decorations loomed up from the walls. It was an exodus in time to
music, which was irresistible to the dedicated ducktail. With
Minie next to him, he immediately found the dance step that
would make procession acceptable to the watching teen-agers
as well.

The stark eyes saw one picture after another: the counters
scintillating with goods; a hundred hostile eyes, fixed on him;
dancing teen-agers with churning bodies crossing and recross-
ing his field of vision; papier-mâché dolls on the walls; stairs
spiraling up to the dome; a circle of faces anxiously watching
for his death; and straight in front of him the reflection in a
glass of the rope on which he had hung. It was the last exodus
of the dying thief as the procession went past Captain Demosthenes de Goede. He had managed to steal his life as well, right
in front of the eyes of the law. The bottle of *Onyx* cologne
fell out of his hands and drenched his clothes; the tie was pulled

over his face to cover the staring eyes; the odor of sanctity rose up against the death mask of Bee-Bee-Doo, enlarged a hundred times, above the exit through which the procession disappeared.

The voice of the little man in white came through the hall; he was reading aloud from a letter that Bee-Bee-Doo had written before her death to Molly Muggeridge, the chatterbox: "Do you remember me? I am Bee-Bee-Doo . . ."

He pointed his stick at the giant-size photo of Bee-Bee-Doo laid out in her copper coffin in the Chamber of Remembrance, dressed in white like a moon goddess, her limbs soft and round, as massaged by Haven & Heller. Her eyes were closed; she seemed to be lying in a copper bath, the paint still wet on her face, her skin damp with all the lotions; the sunlight seemed to have been caught at the window and swallowed up in the structure of death.

The little man put his stick down and resumed his speech. "She drank from the cup of fornication," he said. He looked at all those who had gathered around him and struggled to get his message across to them. He rubbed his mustache and swallowed some lukewarm tea. Angrily he turned on the crowd.

"She had to mill around in filth because we were sick. She had to watch her own downfall . . ." He could scarcely find words. He looked straight at Captain Demosthenes de Goede.

"The struggle of every one of us is revealed in the sickness of the queen. She died like a moon bitch. You had to break her to get at the precious contents."

He pointed to the Gudenov dome.

"The Queen is dead, long live the King!" he jeered.

He spat contemptuously in the direction of everyone, while his anger flared up, and it took a couple of people to subdue him. There were a few chaotic moments until the little man suddenly calmed down and turned his back on them all. Then he fought loose and picked up his stick. He smoothed the creases from his uniform and moved to the next portrait.

"Out of the chaos, darkness and weakness, comes a new light," he said, looking up, and his eyes softened with love for the invisible Bee-Bee-Doo covered with flowers in her copper coffin. "There is a certain Power, and an unfathomable Silence. It comes from above and from below, and in the meeting lies our salvation . . ."

*

Captain Demosthenes de Goede moved blindly through the shopping center with the dedicated ducktail and Minie at his side and the herd of adoring girls at his heels. The anger that was piling up in him at everything that was invisible and obscure was evident from the mighty muscles bulging inside his shirt sleeves, and the veins swelling on his forehead. He looked like Michelangelo's "Moses," and his eyes, like the eyes of the statue, were hewn from marble.

They moved lower and lower down the shopping center to where the lights were dimmer and the atmosphere stranger. He forced his way through the increasing crowds who blocked his path in the search that became more and more hopeless. Now and then the ducktail twanged his guitar and accompanied their strides with the hit beat of the moment; under her teen age hairdo, Minie's eyes were vacant, with the vacancy of one who understood the secrets of the times.

He thought about his mighty past and all the tasks he had performed in the police force, while the dedicated ducktail plucked his base strings to the tune of "Peter Gunn": wit against wit, might against might, order against chaos, where the final outcome was visible in clear relief. He longed for the majestic path of suffering in his past; he longed for shining steel that could draw warm blood; for the simplicity of torturing effort; and for the sharp dividing line of danger, where the choice between dying a noble death and living a noble life was the only option. For one moment the Captain wanted to give in to despair and the catatonic state of vacillation, but at the last moment the surge of purifying anger rose in him, and he resumed his search with renewed energy for the mysterious confusion that was Gudenov.

They found the little man in white, exhausted, in the last stages of the job to which he had given a meaning. He was brewing tea in a little copper dish, abandoned and alone under a huge photograph of Bee-Bee-Doo's grave with its single flower-bedecked stone covering her in the artists' plot, while her body melted away in a bath of posthumous corruption. They looked at him concentrating silently above the flame: a small alchemist filled with the spirit of the anthropos; a little man in the uniform of the shopping center who had, with his own eyes, seen putrefaction and mortification, who was filled with the melancholy of the one who understood, who had become part of the drama of death and suffering, and who waited in vain for rebirth.

He looked up at the Captain, at the mighty Demosthenes de Goede who now stood in front of him, and in the chaos still remained an impotent part of the chaos. He looked longingly up at the Captain. He wanted to see in him someone who understood, like the sun who drove away the darkness, like the setting sun who united with his moon goddess so that after their mutual death, he could appear again, bright and strong on the horizon with the promise of glorious, rapturous life.

He bent despondently over his brew as the dedicated duck-tail's laugh rang through the room and raised a faint echo from the clown in the distance. It was the triumph of the hound, the black wolf. There was no fructification.

The flame burnt under the pot, throwing raven shadows on his face, and reached a fierce heat that threatened any minute to blow everything up. The little man patiently attended to his job, for he was old and had learned the patience of age. He believed that with each repetition something new was created: there were no two souls alike, no two creatures, two plants, two experiences, two misfortunes. One day — one day the sign would appear: crystals like stars on the surface, a mauve light that would glow fluorescently in the dark, a purity that would drive away the darkness and would bathe the whole world in radiance, as an elixir of life, like the sun.

He did not look at the Captain again. There was always tomorrow. Tomorrow he would explain the image of Bee-Bee-Doo all over again, as he did every day of every month of every year — and he would recount the story with devotion and conviction and honesty and candor, even though the result would be disillusionment and loneliness. For he believed in his wares — in Bee-Bee-Doo who had become his own. He believed in the same way that his forefathers had believed in their religion. He would hold the matrix up before them all until fruition took place — perhaps with one of the teen-agers, perhaps with someone who was free from the overpowering conceit. And then . . . His face beamed in the light of the flame.

But meanwhile, he must live. He brewed his tea and added something that he had bought from one of the druggists of the shopping center. He beckoned to the teen-agers lurking in the shadows, and offered them each a sip, right in front of the Captain, who would have arrested the lot if he had understood. They came with their cups in an excited group and received the tea spiced with Purple Heart which they hoped would spur the pale-eyed girls on to love. They each paid him one rand per cup until the copper pot was empty, and then the little man packed up his belongings in his trunk, took off his white coat, put his glasses in his inner pocket, tucked his trousers into his socks and walked with his thermos flask and his baggage to the basement to find his bicycle which would take him to the hole in the city where little men with little jobs made their home.

*

The numbers in the basement of the shopping center seemed to be increasing. The Captain, moving from hall to hall, thought that the whole world, as he knew it, seemed to be meeting here. An intense feeling of melancholy came over the man of action. He had to pronounce judgment on himself, because he was himself part of secular humanity. The hound was an apparition in a nightmare; it lived in the supernatural. (He listened to Bee-Bee-Doo's song which pursued him and roused evasive memories.) But in spite of the invisible, half-familiar ideas that haunted him, there were only the tangible, existential things that repeatedly confronted him. He was overcome by a feeling of ineffable sadness, the by-product of an undefined sin, and there was no solution to be found in the rational, humanistic ideas of the shopping center. He began to have doubts about everything he had achieved in the past, while he wandered around aimlessly; he began to doubt his own powers, and worst of all, the mystery of the enigmatical, unknown power that had always enabled him to rise above the usual and achieve the unusual. He felt like an athlete who had lost his sense of timing, like a champion whose throne had begun to totter, and who could not understand what was going on.

Something was dead. Something had died at some stage or other, and there was nothing left. Captain Demosthenes de Goede had his roots in a heroic tradition; he could fight against mythological monsters; his enemy was discernible against a Gothic background. But in Boris Gudenov's shopping center, as dangerous and as powerful as any primordial specter, he was as impotent as the victims of Medusa.

Something within you is being destroyed; you look at the dangerous object, and you become part of the apostasy that turns you to stone by means of an inescapable, autogenous logic.

If he could only find the hound, the black wolf! He looked around him and saw all the bizarre phenomena which masked the demoniac, but everything was immediately traced back to the humanitarian ethics of the situation, which explained away and justified anything. A feeling of dread took possession of him; he looked all around and became conscious of a Hell that consisted only of alienation, an inability to compromise with the clearly perceptible, with yourself and with those nearest you. And the hound was somewhere, hidden in the commonplace — safer and more inaccessible than in any other hiding place.

The nomination campaign was over, but the bitterness remained; the successful candidates of the trade union bowed their way through the shopping center. Their faces glowed like lighted beacons; they listened happily to grievances and carefully toned down their promises. They disappeared into corners where urgent conversations were held and a new hierarchy came into being. Rogues and scoundrels also came into their own in the democratic acquiescence.

There were numerous conference rooms in the shopping center where politicians, businessmen, technologists and officials held their conferences. Bills and regulations were drawn up while individual rights died easily. There were pharmacies everywhere where procreation could be prevented, remorse stilled and temporary rejuvenation be bought. Somewhere a great clock struck the passing quarter hours. Girls in minidresses were doomed to walk forever because they found it impossible to sit. There were tables full of beads and violently colored garments in a boutique where young men with hair hanging on their shoulders dreamed up far-fetched ensembles for the women. In one of the halls, in a purple light, a girl on a stage was doing a striptease in front of the invisible eyes of the men in the dark. Her garments were strewn all around, you could count her ribs, her feminine secrets were exposed to a roll of drums, and she looked small and confused in the anticlimax of revelation without mystery. In a room next door there was a meeting of right-wingers who thought of all possible precautions to counteract degeneration from the left and, dressed like crows in conservative black, tried to establish, by means of censorship, the dividing line between what was permissible and what was not. There were advertisements on the walls, gambling halls, op art and pop art, roulette tables, showrooms for cars that hit the ton, artificial flowers, field glasses, photometers, antiques, pottery, wigs, cigarette holders, ballpoint pens, fruit, vegetables, cheese, buttons, artificial nails, pets, tours, flags, herbs, copper goods, racquets, golf balls, knives, guns, toys, purgatives, antacid tablets, beer, wine, brandy, books, brooches, diamonds, pearls, batik work, curling pins, crash helmets, windshield wipers, ball bearings, sculpture, paint, wallpaper, earrings, newspapers, flowers, ferns, must, Christmas trees, men's suits, ties, riding breeches, garden chairs, umbrellas, tents, underpants, pliers, scissors, taps, bidets, soap, barometers, theater tickets, writing paper, bush shirts, gray geraniums, red wild chestnut, Jerusalem flowers, mountain lilies, sinks, refrigerators, ammonia, flypaper, sandpaper, sugar, silk stockings and siphunculata under glass.

Captain Demosthenes de Goede, a mighty athlete, surrounded by the flock of girls, accompanied by the dedicated ducktail and Minie, walked slowly through everything that Boris Gudenov offered humanity. Years ago he had tracked down the Swine of Dysselsdorp, and his wanderings had taken him through the drab hills of the Little Karroo, in the scorching heat, between the succulents, past the one-man school with the turrets, next to the aloes and prickly pears and the yellow bush with a snake in its branches, through fields of oxalis, clover and cock ostriches, the sky blue above the Lombardy poplars, and under the yellow flowers of the thorn trees and

the snow teeth of their thorns, by water furrows and stinging
nettles, finch nests, crassulae, euphorbias and succulents, back
to De Rust and Meirings Poort, past the church and the
garage, up to the old watermill where the Swine, exhausted
and hungry, cornered in the kloof in the shadow of the mountain, with grimacing mouth and as tough as a badger, came to
his end; but lived on in a Little Karroo legend, related in the
feeble flickering of candles and the moth-filled light of Miller
lamps.

But the black hound was invisible under the scalloped cor-
nice and in the gallop of the ducktail's guitar.

Boris Gudenov was everywhere, but he was like a great
mountain that was too massive to be seen; he loomed over the
shopping center; he was the shopping center; he was the sick
body in which the viruses reigned supreme. Captain Demosthenes de Goede stood towering in the center of things and
watched it all. The Gudenov current could not be held back.
He closed his eyes and listened to the noise, the atonality that
never ceased, the strepitoso of the Gudenov orchestra. He
opened his eyes and saw the swarming, milling, whirling top
of people. He saw Gudenov goods on the counters stretching
into infinity. He felt the chaos that was continuously kept in
motion by some enormous source of energy in which he himself, with his simplicity of heart and thought, became a part of
the discarded past. He listened to Bee-Bee-Doo's song which
plucked at his heartstrings and became part of the bickering
that mocked ritual. He felt the enormous pull of the Gudenov
power that was trying to draw him into the stream, the iron
grip of the invisible hand. He felt the anxiety and the fear that
came from nowhere, that was vested in no single object, that

had no form, image or dimension. Something was robbing him of his senses and he did not know what it was. He looked at the marriage of two idiots taking place in front of him, and he heard the clown laughing.

In Boris Gudenov's shopping center there was a branch of the civic administration that permitted authorized officials to solemnize marriages. In one of the rooms set apart for this special purpose, a magistrate was considering an application to marry, made by two idiots. Both applicants were in possession of a birth certificate; neither was impotent; neither was certified as abnormal by a medical practitioner. But . . .

Her eyes crossed; her shoulders faced each other; she had nipples but no breasts; she had a mentality hardly above that of an animal; her sex organs functioned with an efficacy that would have roused the jealousy of a sex queen. She was incredibly ugly; she walked in fits and starts; she jerked like an old Ford car; her wasted body was draped in a floral dress; her deformed hands were accoutered to the elbow with snow white gloves on which she had spent her entire dowry; her crooked mouth drooled with unearthly happiness, her fossilized teeth showed in a wide death's head grin.

Her husband, an idiot with a perfect body, testified his moronic benevolence toward the whole world and his bride by a smile that was never switched off. They only touched on the fringe of reality; they were demanding what was proper, decent and respectable. She looked like a witch; he looked like Apollo; and their marriage was solemnized in front of hundreds of people from the shopping center.

Everyone laughed at and cried over the grotesque couple. The teen-agers hummed Bee-Bee-Doo's song softly and swung the rhythm lightly as they watched yet another spectacle from the "gone" world.

When they had to sign the forms and register, neither could do so.

"The . . . papers . . . are . . . important," she said to him, and he smiled in reply.

The magistrate told them to go to a small table where they had to make a mark: an involuntary sign, a *teth* or *tav* as determined by the Unseen Elect. The laughing idiot put his hand over hers, and with spasmodic movements they pushed the pen over the paper until a mark appeared — born from the depths of their combined psyches — an ancient sign that predicted life or death for the two of them.

This travesty was too much for the Captain. Something broke inside him, and he was prepared to hit everyone and everything to pieces; he would fight the whole shopping center indiscriminately, without regard to persons, and in the total destruction would also destroy the invisible hound.

Then the dedicated ducktail spoke up.

"God is dead," he said. "It's man who counts. There is no right or wrong except in relation to context." The ducktail twanged the guitar as though he could hear the truth in the instrument. "The question is whether those two love each other. You must reserve your judgment until you have the picture."

The Captain turned on the ducktail. He saw the two in front of him: Minie hanging onto her dedicated companion who was all the time improvising on his instrument like a calypso singer.

The Captain's broad hands suddenly shot out and grabbed

the young man; he shook him backward and forward so that the guitar skidded away on the floor. There was something in violence that brought a momentary certainty — even if he had to answer to Brigadier Ornassis E. later on. He lifted the dedicated ducktail with one hand and shook him like a dog; he shoved him under his left arm and with his right hand stuffed his mouth with tinsel lying about everywhere on the tables. He throttled him until Minie pulled his arm, and he walked with him through the hall to the outside door. The daylight made the ducktail blink. At first he attempted to struggle, but he was completely vanquished. Then he began to plead and tried to bring the Captain to his senses, until the latter suddenly let him go, turned his back on him, and with dangerous calm surveyed the whole scene in the shopping center.

Demosthenes de Goede began to move slowly through the hall, shattering a fashion dummy or an ornament at every step with a mighty sweep of the hand. The women screamed and the men tried to protect them, but gave way before the demented eyes of the tall figure. Captain Demosthenes de Goede was fighting against the entire shopping center. He was in the grip of a power that had mastered his ego. He was fighting against things that he could not see and could not understand, but he fought. By doing so he was attempting to give a shape to all those invisible things. As he sowed havoc, he saw the red, the yellow and the black faces of Satan. He smashed the faces. The pretty girl in front of him was the daughter of Cenchreis, who made a travesty of love while her mother was on a pilgrimage — and he hit her out of his field of vision. He was halted by three giant figures, huge clumsy wrestlers, who were private detectives and had to keep order in the shopping center. Captain Demosthenes de Goede tackled them. He hit out with his fist at their primitive faces, at their grinning stupidity, brainlessness and primitiveness, reliving his fight with Adam Kadmon Silberstein — and then he was rid of them. He fought against twisters, deceivers, traitors and all who were stained with the sickness of the times, and the floor began to look like a battlefield. His fists were bloodstained, and he found relief in the chaos that he had created. He looked at the scene of wretchedness, and slowly turned back to the door where the dedicated ducktail was being revived by Minie, but he took no notice of them. He left the shopping center and, looking at the sunlit activities in the street, he saw a silver-gray Rolls-Royce slowly moving along a side street.

Suddenly light dawned. There was the man who looked like him! The hound was someone like himself. His bewildered mind saw logic in it: his estranged thinking now recognized the figure that he could not find. He ran up the street before he realized the futility of his action. He suddenly became calm, and his mind now worked with a cunning that lent purpose to his conduct. He got into a car and connected the wires under the dashboard. He started the motor and followed the Rolls-Royce which was disappearing around a bend in the distance. His police training now stood him in good stead. He kept the right distance, not too close, not too far behind. He could see the driver's cap, and also the figure of a woman in the back seat. He now had Boris Gudenov and one of his trollops in his field of vision. He could feel his anger piling up as he thought of all the scorn and mockery he had had to endure while his enemy was all the time watching him like an insect. The moment of revenge had come. Captain Demosthenes de Goede was ready to stake his whole future.

There was one price that no one would pay for life. There were moments in one's life when you had to think for yourself and accept the results of your actions. It would not be a blind onslaught as it had been a while back; he now had the enemy in his sight. It would be his offering to mankind.

As he followed the Rolls-Royce out of the town along the marine drive, past the fishing harbor, beneath the slopes of the mountain where the forest had burned away so that only black stumps showed through the grass and heather, he thought of his wife and children and experienced anew that feeling of anxiety and sadness that he had had at the beginning — a feeling that they were forever beyond his reach. As the two cars approached the Chapman's Peak bend, high above the blue ocean, he realized in his present state of megalomania that that would be one of the sacrifices he would have to make in this task — his greatest, the destruction of Boris Gudenov and all those invisible forces that were ravaging the world. There was a moment of truth as he brought the car up to the Rolls-Royce which, reflecting the sun, was turning the corner at the highest point of the precipice, sheer above the sea. Then at the precise, calculated moment he shot forward and hit the other car. He did not even look around when he heard the screaming of the tires; he drove on slowly while the little side wall broke, and the screams rose above the glorious scenery. He was not positive, but he thought he could even hear the crash in the ocean below, the dull noise of the blue water which, as always, was ready to receive the refuse from the land.

He drove on slowly to the first beach. Some time later, he returned to the scene, where sensation-seekers had already collected for the enjoyment of experiencing the violent death of someone else. The police had halted the traffic; there, where the crowd was at its densest, the bodies were lying in wait for the ambulance which could be heard approaching in the distance, its siren echoing off the slopes of the mountain. Captain Demosthenes de Goede, in perfect control of himself, stood watching the scene. He moved in among the people, but kept putting off the moment when he would have to look at his defeated enemy. He heard the women chattering.

"There is nothing left of the car. They had to pull them up with ropes. It was the most terrible sight I have ever seen. I'll never sleep tonight."

An old woman standing next to Demosthenes de Goede took him for someone who had just arrived on the scene.

"She was still alive," she told him. "Even the last moment before she died, she was thinking of her husband. She called his name over and over." The old woman imitated her in a falsetto voice. "She called 'Boris! Boris! Boris!'" She pulled at Demosthenes de Goede's shirt-sleeve. "Isn't it terrible?"

The Captain decided to go nearer. From years in the police service, he had become hardened to inescapable human suffering. There was no sense in waiting any longer: he would look at his enemy, and then report back to Brigadier Ornassis E. He pushed his way through the sensation-seekers, and forged his way right up to where the remains were lying.

He first saw the chauffeur's cap, and then the man himself. Then he looked at the woman and the four children, and at first he did not seem to understand. He looked for fully a minute before it penetrated, and then he gave a scream that was drowned by the sirens of the ambulance appearing around the corner. But when the sirens stopped, there was no sound from the Captain. His mouth remained open, and his vocal cords were tensed together, but there was complete silence. The bystanders gaped at him curiously and nudged each other, while someone giggled nervously in the sudden hush.

Two men came and took the Captain by his arms. To their surprise, the two members of the action front had no trouble in bringing the huge Captain to their car. They sat on either side of him, and only kept their hands on his arms to prevent him from doing something rash.

*

Retraite.

Brigadier Ornassis E., surrounded by his silent young men of the personnel group and the action front, sat listening to the stuttering Captain who stood before him. They found difficulty in understanding the words, but after a while they got used to it and were able to put some meaning to them.

Captain Demosthenes de Goede was reciting all the tasks that he had achieved, one after the other. They all listened attentively to the account given in ragged words.

"The Lesbian Poisoner of Calvinia," came with difficulty.

"The Swine of Dysselsdorp . . ."

"The Serpent of Muldersvlei . . ."

"The Blackmailer of Arcadia . . ."

"The Sweetheart of Kammaland . . ."

"The Lion of the North . . ."

"The Bull of Benoni . . ."

"The Whores of Humansdorp . . ."

Then the Captain stopped suddenly. He seemed to be struggling with his memory, and his tongue seemed to be entangled when it came to the next sentence. The Brigadier leaned forward to hear better. After a moment's struggle, the words came. "The Hound of . . . ," but he could not find the next word. "Shopping center" lay quite beyond the capabilities of his stammering tongue.

There was no stopping the Captain; he kept on talking, although most of the sentences were quite unintelligible. He was trying to give an account of his life in the service of humanity; he told it calmly, and his narrative seemed to have no end.

The Brigadier turned to one of the young men of the personnel department, and said that he was worried about the Captain's unnatural calm. It was an extremely dangerous symptom pointing to an explosive condition. He interrupted the Captain's report, and the latter listened very submissively. He confirmed all the tasks the Captain had performed; on behalf of everyone, he expressed his thanks for his unselfish service and the sacrifices that had been necessary. He became more and more eloquent as he gained control of the situation. "We must remember that disintegration is not the fault of the individual, but of fate over which we have no control."

He smoothed his hair with his hand, and nodded to his young men to relax.

"After a full life," said the Brigadier, leaning forward sympathetically and looking the Captain straight in the eye, "after a full life everyone comes to the crossroads, where he has to decide what to do with the rest of his life. Should he find release from the moment of tragedy (everyone's lot at some time or other) in self-destruction, or should he look for reassurance in life which is often incomprehensible but which always remains a task and a challenge?" Brigadier Ornassis E.

seemed to have a sudden brain wave, and he looked quickly at his young men of the personnel group to see if they were ready to grasp this special refinement:

"Must not one accept torment as perhaps the greatest of all tasks? Is there not perhaps a thirteenth task, not on the record, that everyone ventures upon alone, this time for his own sake? Does true greatness perhaps not lie in the victory about which no one hears? Is the acceptance of life as it is, even if it is without the help and understanding of the supernatural, not a triumph in itself?"

The Brigadier had now even forgotten the Captain.

"Is the patient acceptance of bare existence, such as belongs to the least of humans, not perhaps the greatest victory? Is it a crime against yourself to become part of the times and to be content with the shoddy existence of humanity?"

The men of the personnel department looked up strangely at the Brigadier who, as so often in the past, was in a mysterious way going over to enemy. But they knew from bitter experience that the Brigadier always knew best.

"We shall find our salvation in joining our love with the mere fact of our existence," said the Brigadier. "Boris Gudenov is not our enemy. It was just a cunning game of the invisible enemy which the Captain revealed to us."

At once he became short and businesslike.

"There has been a change of policy. It must be accepted as such. Traditional images must be destroyed. The Service must be modernized. There is a radically new approach supported by the best brains. The image of Boris Gudenov must be reconstructed. That is an order to the personnel department; it is the duty of the action front to execute it."

And now he turned again to the Captain.

"I think the Captain has the courage to choose life rather than release through death. The D-Service has the honor, Captain, to invite you to spend the rest of your days in the Welgevonden Foundation. Thanks to the vision of Jock Silberstein, a progressive Jew, you will be able to find peace and quiet on the property that he has put at the disposal of the community."

*

Captain Demosthenes H. de Goede was driven in a brand-new Cadillac, belonging to the D-Service, to the Welgevonden Institute where a cottage was prepared for his special use. This was where he had met Hope, where he had performed his first task, where Mrs. Dreyer would predict peace for the rest of his life.

He was perfectly happy when he saw the familiar scenes. The glass house flashed an exuberant welcome in the sun. It was here that he had overcome the Giant, Adam Kadmon Silberstein, and destroyed the last traces of primordial phenomena.

For the rest of his life he would enjoy the ephemeral design and be free of the curse of suffering, love, grief and creation.

THE THIRD EYE

Burn, tycoon, burn! · When Katy
and her friends heard the screams, they
ran to the room, but their way was blocked
by the plate glass door that was locked on the inside. Through the glass they saw the terrible suffering of
the great man who totally ignored the observers — the crowds
who banged the glass in vain and milled around helplessly.
The hostess and her companions, rejuvenated by synthetic
estrogen, their love life infinitely prolonged, looked at this
form of suffering in bewilderment and incomprehension. He
was not someone like them; there had always been something
like the glass between them; his attention had always been
focused on himself alone; he had never really been part of
the community; there had always been that contradiction in
his makeup; he had his own places of refuge; he was a sort of
aristocrat; snobbish, actually; he understood women in a way
that was completely unacceptable to them.

Katy's friends led her away to spare her further suffering.
They took her to her room while she deplored her own part
in the disaster that had befallen their house. They comforted
her by referring to her own blameless life, an example of self-
sacrifice and good intentions. Could she help it if she could
not foresee the results of her innocent gesture?

While she wept on one shoulder after another and, with a
slight movement, let her hair fall loose on her shoulders, while
her face contorted with a grief that immediately commands
attention from all women and help from all men, while she
leaned fragilely on her companion's shoulder, she asked them
to keep the gesture secret, for the whole world would read
guilt into the innocence of her deed. Silence would protect
her, silence would expunge the shame.

They could no longer look at such suffering. They comforted her on the way to her room, where she sank down on the bed with a sob of sorrow. Nothing had any meaning for her now: her marriage bed that would always be empty; her house; the mockery of wealth that could no longer offer any comfort. What was left to her except death, because was she not really dead?

They hastened to make her abandon that idea.

She lay pale on the bed; a small womanly figure, tortured beyond the limits of human endurance.

They watched over her the whole night. Over their fragile, vulnerable — no, wounded friend.

They pointed out that a new life lay ahead of her, in which she would have to play the role of the man; in which she would be able to serve the community by means of the infinite variety of this source of power.

They talked to her until she ceased weeping; in her hour of sorrow they showed her things that she had not understood in the past; by a kind of dialectic process they managed in her suffering to break up those personifications that had so confused her in the past; they created a bridge; by means of the shock of what had happened, they made her become aware of the psychic processes as they understood them; they made her see the light in the glow of the burning tycoon.

*

The left eye.

Iole also heard the cry from where she was lying under the art treasures, a sacrificial victim, destroyed and bleeding. Something was struggling with itself: a feeling that everything was in a state of reconstruction; that in destruction there was also

victory. She herself was the refractor. She had received the
original light, which was fading, and she had doused it in her
feminine fluid. She had damped down the scorching heat with
her moistness. She had enabled her invisible lover to die.
While she listened to the cries in the distance, she was already
beginning to feel the satisfying regeneration after weakness
and impotence. It felt as though she, a young woman, with
infinite wisdom became aware of a deeper significance within
herself, a greater truth; You are I; I am you; on earth and in
heaven; for all time — I on your left hand, you on my right —
and we float through the night and the stars to meet the day
— and the two halves become one — and the sun suddenly
shines brightly over this barren landscape with rays that are
blinding to the eyes — and there are flowers growing in the
wilderness, and the whole desert is alive with colors that
stretch over the plains like an Arabian carpet, right up to the
slopes of the Swartberg — and we raise a song of praise to the
All-Knowing Forefather — and something new is born in us
that is both man and woman, enfolding everything doublefold
— and suddenly the clown has stopped laughing, for sorrow
is truth, and the whole world is singing the song . . .

of which Bee-Bee-Doo's song was only a tormenting in-
timation, and whose refrain was unconsciously repeated in the
teen-agers' noise that had the dissonance of an unformed sigh

and it lived in the computer that calculated the song and
could not destroy the truth even in its monstrous product —
for in the banality of the present lay the mutilated truth of the
past

and tragedy is relieved of the tragic by the certainty of rebirth

— and Iole listened in the triumph of her one and only love

to the cries of her invisible lover who was finding release in the burning flame above Oita.

*

The right eye.

There was something that burned more fiercely than the fiery garment; there was something that caused more pain than scorched flesh; there was a greater agony than self-chastisement. It was the numinosity of the images that came from deep and far. He could forgive those figures behind the glass; their guilt or innocence was no longer important. Even the irony of their vengeance faded before the deeper vision. He thought of everything he had achieved and all the tasks he had performed which were beyond the ordinary man. But he eschewed reproach and natural self-pity, which at that moment lost their hold on him. Even in the agonizing pain he could discern the protection of a deeper insensitivity. Something greater than human reactions spoke within him; a greater knowledge intensified his isolation. The struggling body, the screams and the signs of external torment were not a true reflection of the calm within. He saw his ghastly reflection in the mirror, but something raised him above the earthly and the material. The flame flickered and he was free no longer, an exalted loneliness came over him, everything became impersonal, and something spoke within him.

He saw the menorah on the prayer standard, he saw the four pillars of the holy ark and the wise old men reading from the sacred books. Whatever it was that had blocked the memories of the far past had disappeared in the flames. He was aware of his soul; he felt the presence of the *Shekinah*. There was a gold chain binding him to his far endless past. The mantle of the Baal-Shem, who could understand the Wise Name, gave meaning to the flames that were burning it; the seven candles, that had set it alight, united him with Hermes Trismegistus in the consuming flame. And he saw his mother, her embroidered shawl about her shoulders, who had wept that Sabbath evening when she had lit the candles and could see an image of the future in the far away *schtetl.*

Boris Gudenov burned in the form of a cross, with his arms outstretched on either side. He burned in front of young Hyllus who peered from behind the glass door, and in all the spectacles of the evening had seen things that would haunt him for the rest of his life, although there would be nothing in his education to help him to give them meaning.

Meanwhile his father, the tycoon, burned behind the glass until there was nothing recognizable left. And the millions and all the dreadful responsibilities connected with them became the heritage of himself and his beloved mother who would use the wealth for worthy causes, social services and art exhibitions, and everything that was looked upon with favor by the state, the community and the world of science.

*

The Brigadier's eyes.

Brigadier Ornassis E. sat on the topmost floor of the Oita shopping center and meditated, surrounded by his young men of the D-Service, while he listened to a built-in automatic organ playing "The End of a Perfect Day." The girls had already filled the glasses, and they all waited for the Brigadier to propose the toast as soon as he had completed his reverie.

The room was filled, not only with the staff of the Service, but also with many teen-agers, officials from the shopping center, clients and relatives of the tycoon. As soon as the last notes died away, with tremolo effects, the Brigadier stood up. He closed a book of new verse by the great poet and put it down on the table next to him. "The gods are great and lonely in the night, and hang like yellow fruit on the trees," he quoted softly to his young men of the personnel service who formed a tight phalanx around him. He let his hands rest on two broad shoulders, and bowed his head.

"But I peer down in the small shaft of this sunlight . . ."

He was dressed in the black clothes of a business executive, his tie was silver gray with a cultured pearl pin. He surveyed his audience thoughtfully, then raised his eyes to a chandelier with thousands of crystals that glittered in the light.

"Tonight," he said, "I am paying tribute to Boris Gudenov, beloved ex-enemy, unhonored prophet, salt of the earth." He waited until the applause died down, then took a sip from the glass in his hand. "But my friends, I want you to see him, not as he was at the end, dying in weakness and estrangement, but as the man he was." He looked at Katy, her lady friends, and at Hyllus, the Peeping Tom. "And I wish to express my sincere sympathy to the family who must now spend the rest of their lives without the great man, but who, thanks to circumstances, were spared the last moments of deterioration." He nodded in the direction of the family (unknown uncles, cousins and relatives from Mezeritz, Podolia, Bratzlaf and Videbsk).

"Allow me to confess that our Service, with the help of the celebrated Captain Demosthenes de Goede, set itself the task of destroying what we in our ignorance did not realize was the truth." He took out his handkerchief and sniffed delicately at the perfume. "And my friends, in order to bring the truth to light for us, Captain Demosthenes de Goede had to sacrifice his own family — perhaps the greatest sacrifice that can be asked of anyone." He put his handkerchief away. "Just as Boris Gudenov's family, in a reverse manner, had to make their sacrifices."

He waited a moment and looked at the crowd. What he now had to say was a difficult idea to grasp. "There were two forces, my friends, concerned in the struggle. There was Bee-Bee-Doo . . ." As soon as a few began to clap, especially the man in white, the young men of the D-Service silenced them, and the pretty girls from Clifton placed their fingers coyly on their lips to guarantee silence. "There was Bee-Bee-Doo," repeated the Brigadier, "a vulgar relic of the primitive, someone who really should have been in a sanatorium. There was the ritual and mystery that for us ordinary folk became a source of doubt and suspicion. And I am glad to say that many of our spiritual leaders understand." He nodded to a couple of bishops who smiled and nodded back. "Dare I mention that even the wife of our beloved Captain, with the ironic name of Hope, also played an unfortunate part in the confusion of ideas? Was it divine vengeance that she had to become the victim because of her complicity?" He looked expectantly at the young men of the personnel division, who with loud No's immediately fell in with the Brigadier's new image. He smiled. "I am glad to see that all of you, as ordinary people, have immediately appreciated the truth." He smiled at the teen-agers who, mystified, retained their mask of aloofness. "No. She was the victim of an illness, nymphomania, for which, we hope, a cure will be found one of these days." He smiled at the doctors, who laughed in reply. "Dare I admit that I was also a victim? That with the arrogance of the Demiurge I saw myself as a companion?" Only a few young men of his Service laughed at the Brigadier's slip of referring at this stage to an idea like the Demiurge.

The Brigadier had emptied his glass and held it out for one of the young men of the action front to refill.

He laughed at the audience, who laughed back.

"May I mention someone by name who gave us the true picture, a former assistant of Boris Gudenov, who had to accept chastisement patiently, and who, with typical neighborly love, carried no vengeance in his heart? May I mention someone known as the ducktail?"

There was much laughter as the ducktail, beloved by all, came forward and strummed the Watusi on his guitar, until the teen-agers automatically went through the movements, while the Brigadier looked on good-naturedly and made use of the opportunity to refill his glass.

"Can there be a greater triumph," asked the Brigadier, "than the realization that God is dead, and that man, freed from traditional bondage, can build his life purely on Christian morality?"

He faced the audience squarely.

"Is this gathering not an indication of greater understanding, greater freedom and neighborly love?"

"That was the message of Boris Gudenov, my friends," said the Brigadier with deep conviction. "And both the Captain and our beloved tycoon had to end their separate careers to demonstrate this truth."

He suddenly stood up.

"The Captain, a man like us, misled as I myself was in the heroic tradition, had to go through the valley of the shadow of death and be reconciled with the secular truth. Dare we judge him if he became a victim of this particular situation; should we not rather admire him as he experiences his greatest triumph when he accepts this world and, in the progressive Welgevonden, becomes absorbed in the new world? As people with an understanding of the new symbols that get a new value through reality and existentialism, dare we judge Boris Gudenov when at the last moment, as a result of physical suffering, he accepted the primitive significance that is completely a mockery of his enlightened bulwark, the shopping center?"

The Brigadier had now reached the end of his speech, and he smiled at the girls of the Service who were prepared to receive the men on purely humanistic grounds — sex as sex, love as love, truth as truth as everyone saw it at that moment.

There was new life in the Service.

The Brigadier smiled.

There was a new picture, and he raised his glass. They all drank the toast eagerly. Goodwill and neighborly love had simplified life, so that everyone could understand. They drank to the death of tradition and primordial life. There was much gaiety and freedom, and rejoicing without limits.

Death was no longer in the building, and the Brigadier was satisfied to sit down in the Renaissance chair while they all joined in the revels, and organ music from invisible sources interpreted the new truth with a clash of sound.